A FUNNY DIRTY LITTLE WAR

Osvaldo Soriano

A FUNNY
DIRTY LITTLE WAR

translated by Nick Caistor

readers international

The title of this book in Spanish is *No habrá más penas ni olvido*,
first published in Spanish in Barcelona by Editorial Bruguera in 1980,
and subsequently by Bruguera, Buenos Aires, 1983,
by Seix Barral, Barcelona, 1985, and by
Editorial Sudamericana, Buenos Aires, 1986.

First published in English by Readers International, Inc., London
and New York, whose editorial branch is at
8 Strathray Gardens, London NW3 4NY, England.
US/Canadian inquiries to Subscriber Service Department,
P.O. Box 959, Columbia, Louisiana 71418 USA.

Cover illustration and design by the Argentinian artist Oscar Zarate

Typeset by Grassroots Typeset, London NW6
Printed and Bound in Great Britain by Richard Clay
(The Chaucer Press) Ltd., Bungay, Suffolk

ISBN 0-930523-17-2 Hardcover
ISBN 0-930523-18-0 Paperback

to the memory of my father

PART ONE

Mi Buenos Aires querido
cuando yo te vuelva a ver
no habrá más penas ni olvido.

Buenos Aires my love,
When I return to your shore,
Pain and longing shall be no more.

—Carlos Gardel

'YOU got infiltrators,' said the Inspector.

'Infiltrators? The only person who works here is Mateo, and he's been at the Town Hall for twenty-four years.'

'You're infiltrated. I'm warning you, Ignacio, get rid of him, there's going to be problems.'

'Who's to cause problems? I'm Council Leader, and you and me, we've known each other for years. So who's going to stir up trouble?'

'The Regulator.'

'The who?'

'Suprino. He's back from Tandil with orders to regulate things.'

'Come off it, Suprino's a friend of mine. I sold him my truck a month ago, and he still owes me for it.'

'He's back to restore order.'

'Restore what order? You've been reading too many newspapers.'

'Mateo is a Marxist-Communist.'

'Whoever put that idea in your head? Mateo went to school with us.'

'He's gone over.'

'But all he does is collect the taxes and push around the paperwork.'

'I'm warning you, Ignacio, fire him.'

'How can I? The whole town'd be up in arms.'

'What am I here for?'

'What *are* you here for?'

'To take care of law and order in the town.'

'Come on, do me a favour. Get stuffed.'

'I mean it. Suprino's in the bar. He's going to come and see you, to give you some friendly advice.'

'Tell him to pay me first. Otherwise, I'll report him to you.'

Ignacio walked out of the police station. Two policemen standing under a tree outside the entrance saluted as he left. He got on his bike and pedalled off slowly, deep in thought. Already that morning it was close to a hundred degrees. He slowed down still further as he reached the corner, to let Manteconi's siphon bottle truck pass. Then he cycled on to the next block, in the centre of the town, and came to a halt outside the bar. He left his bike propped in the shade on the sidewalk and went in. He took off his cap and waved a greeting; two old men playing cards grunted in response. He went up to the bar.

'Hello there, Vega. Seen Suprino?'

'He just left. He's in a real state. He went off to see Reinaldo at the Union office. There going to be a strike?'

'Where?'

'Here. That's what Suprino said.'

'Jesus Christ, everybody's gone off their heads. Give me a Coke.' He gulped it down straight from the bottle.

'What's going on, Ignacio?'

'Your guess is as good as mine. What else did Suprino say?'

'Not a lot. That you're going to resign.'

'Me?'

'You and Mateo. He says you're traitors.'

'He said that?'

'Yes.'

'The bastard.'

' "A traitor". Guzman heard him too.'

'What was the auctioneer doing here?'

'I think he was waiting for Suprino. They went over to the Union office together.'

'You know Guzman is no Peronist. We had a scrap over it back in '66.'

'Yes, I remember, in the square.'

'He had me put in jail for being a Peronist when Soldatti was Inspector...How much?'

'Nothing,' Vega said, his broad grin revealing a set of yellow, uneven teeth. 'Not if you're going to be out of work.'

'OK, 'bye.'

Ignacio got on his bike and rode off furiously. A *coup!* A wry smile spread across his face. 'So they think they can teach me to be a Peronist?' A strange elated feeling swept over him. He'd never imagined he'd have to head off an attempted coup, just like Perón, Frondisi, or Illia. He reached the square. He stood the bike against a bench, and walked up to the clump of trees in the middle. It was eleven o'clock, and the heat meant the square was deserted. He sat down on the grass and took out a cigarette.

'How's things, Don Ignacio?' asked the gardener.

'Don't bother me, I'm trying to think. Go do your watering further off.'

He dropped his face in his hands. 'They're trying to cut the ground from under my feet,' he said out loud. Beyond the square, the loudspeakers were blaring with commercials. He took stock. Suprino was Party Secretary. Ignacio had sent him to Tandil the previous day to ask the Mayor to approve the funds for an extension to Colonia Vela's first-aid post. He'd come back full of himself and had managed to involve the Inspector and Guzman in some wild scheme or other. Now they had it in for him. 'But it was me the town voted for. Six hundred and forty votes. What's this crap about Mateo being Communist? He was already working at the Town Hall when Perón got kicked out in '55. He carried on there afterwards — he's always worked there. Nobody ever asked him if he was a Communist. Gandolfo's the bolshie. Has been all his life, and everybody knows it. But he's the ironmonger, and nobody bothers him. He was even on the Residents' Association once. So what on earth is all this infiltration, for God's sake. I'll stick the lot of them in jail, dammit... Hey, Moyano, come here a minute.'

The gardener dropped his hose and scurried over.

'What can I do for you, Don Ignacio?'

'What if I arrested Guzman and Suprino?'

'What have they done, Don Ignacio?'

'They're leading an insurrection.'

'What's that?'

'They want to kick me out.'

'You!'

'Yes. Me and Mateo.'

'But how will Don Mateo get by? His wife's sick, and his daughter's studying in Tandil.'

'They're determined to get rid of us.'

'But why, Don Ignacio?'

'They claim I'm not a Peronist.'

'You not a Peronist?' the gardener guffawed. 'Didn't I see you with my own eyes slugging it out with Guzman right here because you were on Perón's side?'

'I'll have them locked up.'

The old gardener thought for a moment. 'What does the Inspector say to that?'

The question hit Ignacio like a bolt from the blue. He leapt up and ran to his bike.

'Where's the Inspector?'

The prisoner cleaning the doorway looked up and stood to attention.

'Inside, with Deputy Inspector Rossi and the six constables. They took me out of my cell and told me to wash the flag and mop the floor.'

Ignacio went in. There was nobody in the office. He passed through to the yard and saw them. The Inspector stood facing the policemen, with Rossi at his side in his cleanest uniform. Ignacio arrived in time to hear: 'to root out once and for all the treasonous enemy that has infiltrated Colonia Vela...'

'Come to my office, Ruben.'

'Don't give me orders, Ignacio.'

'What on earth are you doing sweating your balls off out here in the heat? Come into the office.'

'I won't. Nobody's going. You're not giving me any more orders, Ignacio. You're a traitor.'

Ignacio realised he meant it. He stared at him a second, then turned on his heel and left. Back in the hallway he went up to the prisoner.

'What's your name?'

'Juan Ugarte, sir.'

'Get over to the Town Hall and wait for me there.'

'Yes, Don Ignacio.'

Ignacio picked up his bike and cycled off. The prisoner ran up the street. It was noon. A shrill, confused shouting was coming over the loudspeakers: 'Compañeros! Compañeros!' Ignacio recognised Reinaldo's voice.

'Compañeros! The Communists in Colonia Vela are refusing our just request for funds for the first-aid post! They are holding up the permit for a monument

6

to Motherhood! They are blocking the installation of drains! Compañeros! We must get rid of the traitors Ignacio Fuentes and Mateo Guastavino! Our workers' General Union and our people's police will together defeat the anarchist plot against Colonia Vela! Stand firm in your support for the Peronist Party Secretary General, Compañero Suprino! Let's teach the Marxist oligarchy a lesson they will never forget!'

Ignacio dug in his heel to stop the bike, and left it against the wall of the store. It was a rambling old house which had been his father's, as had the shop, now run by his wife.

Felisa wrapped the quarter of ham, gave it to a little girl with long braids, then wiped her hands on her apron.

'Just closing, Ignacio. Lunch is almost ready.'

'Can't you hear the loudspeakers?'

'I wasn't really paying attention.'

'There's been a revolution, sweetheart. A revolution against me! Just like against Perón!'

'What are you talking about?'

'Quick, shut the shop.'

Felisa closed both sides of the wooden shop door, and double-locked it.

'Listen, Felisa: I'm going out. Don't open the door to anyone — anyone, understand?'

'Ignacio! What have you done, Ignacio?'

The Council Leader went into the bedroom and took an ancient Smith & Wesson from the chest of drawers. He groped among the carefully folded sheets

7

and collected the bullets. Fifteen in all.

'Bring me the shotgun.'

'No, Ignacio! What're you going to do? They'll kill you!'

'Kill me, those bastards? They're all scared stiff.'

'I'll call Ruben.'

'He's the bastard I'm going to fight.'

Ignacio stuck the revolver in his belt. He slung the shotgun over his shoulder, kissed his wife on the cheek and before stepping outside added: 'If only God had granted me a son to fight alongside his father today.'

The street was deserted. He could make out a confused squawking coming from the loudspeakers six blocks away in the town centre. Ignacio looked around him. 'Shit! They've stolen my bike.' On the wall where it had been leaning, someone had scrawled:

FUENTES A TRAITOR
TO THE PERONIST PEOPLE

'The sons of bitches! I'll shoot my way to the Town Hall!'

Nobody seemed to want to stop him. Ignacio could see old Sarah, the woman who lived across the street, peering at him through her window. Someone hidden in a doorway shouted:

'We're right behind you, Fuentes!'

The heat was unbearable. Ignacio walked to the street corner. He was fifty-one, and had lost too much hair to be out in the sun without a cap. He could feel the sweat on his neck; his shirt was sticking to him under the arms and under the shotgun strap.

'Ignacio!' The shout brought him up short. He turned and saw his wife running towards him. She was carrying a cartridge belt.

'You forgot these.'

He smiled weakly at her. 'Did you bring my cap?'

'No, just the cartridges. I'll go back for it.'

'No. Don't leave the house. Go on.'

He turned into the main street and walked on slowly for two blocks. The town seemed completely empty. When he reached the street where the Town Hall stood, he stopped and looked up and down it before turning the corner. Two policemen were guarding the entrance.

'You two!' Ignacio shouted.

Silence.

'You two cops!'

The policemen peered into the doorways of the nearby houses. They were armed with old machine guns.

'Here, idiots. On the corner.'

They whirled round. Ignacio called out: 'Where's the Inspector?'

'Inspector Llanos has gone to lunch,' one of them shouted back. The loudspeakers had fallen silent. It was one in the afternoon and the whole town was getting ready for a siesta. Ignacio walked on towards the Town Hall. One of the policemen blocked his way.

'I'm sorry. You can't go in.'

'On whose orders?'

'Inspector Llanos's, sir.'

'You, what's your name?'

'Garcia, sir.'

'And you?' addressing the other man.

'Comini, sir. You're not allowed in.'

'Where are the others?'

'Confined to barracks, sir.'

'Hmm... Who do you take your orders from?'

'The Inspector, sir.'

'And if the Inspector isn't there?'

'Deputy Inspector Rossi.'

'And if he's not there?'

The policemen exchanged glances.

'I'm in charge here, dammit! Attention, dammit!' roared Ignacio.

The two clicked their heels.

'Garcia, I'm promoting you to Corporal and giving you a raise. How much do you earn?'

'104,000 after stoppages and with family allowance, Don Ignacio.'

'I'm raising it to 150,000.'

'Thank you, sir!'

'Corporal Garcia!'

'At your orders, sir.'

'Order Constable Comini to go and fetch the gardener.'

'Yes, sir: Constable Comini!'

'Yes, Corporal.'

'Run and get Moyano the gardener. Quick about it!'

'Corporal Garcia!'

'Sir!'

'Come with me and I'll sign your promotion.'

'Yes, sir. Thank you, sir.'

They walked together into the Town Hall. Ignacio closed the front door. Mateo sat hunched over his desk, alone in the office. His face was ashen. When he saw the Council Leader he stood up.

'Don Ignacio! They want to throw us out, Don Ignacio!'

'Here's a shotgun. We're not going to take this lying down.'

'What's going on, Don Ignacio?'

'They claim we're bolshies.'

'Bolshies? What d'they mean? I've always been a Peronist...I never got mixed up in politics.'

'That's what they say. Type me out a form appointing Constable Garcia a corporal, would you?'

Mateo sat at the Olivetti and began to type.

'Corporal Garcia,' said Ignacio. 'We're going to defend the Town Hall. Stand guard by that window over there.'

'Yes, sir.'

Mateo pulled the sheet from the typewriter.

'Will you sign it, Don Ignacio?'

Ignacio signed. Corporal Garcia looked at the piece of paper, and stuck out his chest.

'What's my old woman going to say?' The ends of his bushy moustache almost touched his ears. Comini and the gardener appeared.

'How much do you earn, Moyano?'

11

'About 83,000.'

'I'm appointing you Director of Parks and Gardens, and raising your salary to 120,000.'

'Thank you, Don Ignacio. You can't imagine how much...'

'Corporal Garcia, give him your revolver.'

'What on earth for, Don Ignacio?' Moyano queried.

'So that you can defend the town.'

The gardener didn't understand a word. He took the Ballester Molina and looked quizzically at it. He was close to retirement age, and his hands shook slightly.

'Constable Garcia!'

The booming voice came from the street.

'It's the Inspector,' Garcia said, looking round at Ignacio. 'If he sees me, he'll put me in the clink.'

'Constable Comini!'

'The Inspector's calling me.'

'You're staying here,' Ignacio said.

'If I'm still a constable, I may as well go with him.'

The Inspector was standing in the middle of the street. Behind him were Deputy Inspector Rossi, Guzman the auctioneer, Suprino, Reinaldo, and half a dozen young men. Ignacio poked his head out of the window.

'Come out, Garcia. That's an order.'

'He's spotted me, Don Ignacio. I'm done for.'

'He never did. Don't go out.'

'Garcia!'

'I'm off.'

'Hang on! Who made you a corporal?'

'You did, Don Ignacio, but if I don't go they'll put us all in jail.'

'Don't be a chicken. If you do go, he'll have you anyway for letting me in here.'

'Comini! Come on out, be a man,' shouted the Inspector.

'You stay here,' Garcia bellowed at him.

'You're crazy.'

'You're staying, I tell you.'

'We'll both end up behind bars, Garcia.'

'Corporal Garcia to you.'

'You're not going anywhere,' Ignacio said, pointing his gun at Comini's chest.

'Lock him in the toilet,' he ordered Garcia.

'Hand over your guns.'

Comini dropped his machine gun and his revolver onto the floor, The Corporal pushed him into the w.c. and locked the door.

'What next, Don Ignacio?'

'Get ready to defend your Town Council.'

'Nobody's going to get in here, sir. Moyano, bolt the back door.'

'I don't want to get killed.'

'I'll be the one who kills you if you don't do what I say.'

Moyano looked at him and realised he meant it. He ran to carry out the order.

The Inspector was now on the far pavement. He

was waving his arms about. Rossi saluted, clicked his heels and ran off as fast as he could. Suprino was giving instructions to a group of young men in civilian clothes who were carrying submachine guns and sawn-off shotguns.

The heat and sunlight were bouncing off the road. Rossi came back in the police van and drew it up across the intersection to make a roadblock. Curious passersby began to gather. The loudspeakers started blaring out again: 'Citizens! We men of Colonia Vela are fighting a battle for freedom! Fuentes, a Communist thief disguised in Peronist colours, must be forced out! Together we must flush him out of his nest! Long live Argentina! Long live Colonia Vela! Long live Perón!'

'What the devil's got into them?' Ignacio muttered to himself. 'Mateo, call up the Mayor's office in Tandil.'

'You want to speak to the Mayor?'

'Person-to-person. If he's not there, get him at home. Hurry up, before they cut off the phone.'

Mateo rattled the receiver. The operator asked for the number.

'Put me through to the Mayor, Clarita, quickly.'

'Garcia. Close the shutters. They're bound to use tear gas on us.'

'There isn't any tear gas in the police station, Don Ignacio.'

'Shut them anyway. What's the Inspector up to now?'

14

'Making barricades. The silly old fool is piling up rubbish in the street. He's stealing all the fruit boxes from pegleg Duran's grocery.'

Juan Ugarte came into the office through the back door. Moyano was with him.

'My life for Perón,' whooped Juan.

'Where have you been?' Ignacio asked.

'We were keeping watch from the roof. Like snipers.'

'Snipers!' Ignacio said. 'Good idea. Good idea. Take the revolver and get back up there. Don't shoot unless I give the order.'

'I'm on my way.'

'Hey!'

'Yes, sir?'

'Why were you in jail?'

'For being drunk, to tell the truth. I work at the brick furnace, and every now and then I have a few snorts at old Bustos' place. Whenever a cop catches me, they make me clean out the cells and the rest of the police station. The food they give you is awful, Constable Garcia here can vouch for that....'

'Corporal...' Garcia corrected him. 'I'm a corporal now.'

'Well I never! So you've gone up in the world, *amigo*. I must be off: my life for Perón!'

'Your call, Don Ignacio,' Mateo shouted. The Council Leader ran to the phone.

'Hello? Sr. Guglielmini?'

'I was having my siesta, Fuentes.'

15

'I'm sorry, but the thing is I've got a problem, sir. The Police Inspector and the Party Secretary have mutinied. He claims he's come to regulate...'

'What are you going to do about it?' the Mayor cut in.

'What am *I* going to do about it? What about *you?* I'm holed up in the Town Hall and I need police reinforcements from Tandil.'

'Look, Fuentes, it's your job to look after things in Colonia Vela. Send me a report tomorrow.'

'But you're the Mayor.'

'You're the person under suspicion.'

'Who says?'

'The executive council of the Party. They say Mateo is a Communist and that you're protecting him. That you're all militants, you and those youngsters.'

'What youngsters?'

'Those who fixed the school desks and cleaned up the first-aid post for you. You know who I mean. They're always wandering in and out of your office, like they owned the place...'

'They're good kids, they're helpful and they're Peronists.'

'Peronists, my arse!' Guglielmini hung up abruptly.

Juan came rushing in. His shirt was unbuttoned, and the hairs on his chest were soaked with sweat.

'Don Ignacio, they've raided your house!'

'My house?'

'Yes. They've arrested your wife. They say on the

loudspeaker they found Communist propaganda and arms.'

'Is that what they're saying?'

'Yes. Books by Che Guevara and arms.'

'The air rifle . . . I forgot the air rifle! What's Felisa got to do with all that?'

'I saw them dragging her away, Don Ignacio. Sorry about the bad news.'

Ignacio scratched his head, chewed at his moustache, then growled: 'Right. That does it. I've had a bellyful of their games. Juan, go and find the road gang. Explain to the foreman what's happened and get them all to come with you. No, better still, I'll give it to you in writing. Type it out, Mateo.'

'What am I supposed to do with them?' Juan asked. 'They're only eight or ten old duffers.'

'Form a platoon. They've got picks, shovels, and knives. Take them to the square.'

Garcia was observing the street through the crack. in the window.

'They've spilt Pegleg's fruit all over the place. I reckon they're going to attack.'

'We'll shoot their balls off first,' Ignacio said.

Juan left by the back door. Mateo chimed in: 'I could resign, Don Ignacio. That'd settle matters.'

'You'll do no such thing,' Corporal Garcia said. 'Now you're giving your life for Perón.'

'Your life for Perón,' Ignacio echoed. 'I wonder what Perón is doing at this moment?'

'A lot of people are watching us,' Garcia said, smil-

17

ing. 'All those who voted for us are out there now.'

The Council Leader went over to the window and squinted out of a crack.

'Ignacio Fuentes!' the Inspector shouted through cupped hands. 'Give yourselves up! The Party tribunal will decide your case. Come out and surrender.'

Ignacio pulled back one of the shutters and smashed the glass with his shotgun.

'You surrender. You're the one in revolt.'

'You're the one who encourages police personnel to mutiny. Hand over Garcia and Comini!'

'Come and get them, you fat bastard!'

'The people are my witness! You Communist swine!'

Ignacio let fire with both barrels. The buckshot smacked into the fruit boxes and toppled the barricade. The onlookers fled. The Inspector flung himself to the ground.

'Wow! Will you look at that!' shouted Garcia. The gardener covered his ears. Ignacio reloaded both barrels. Mateo began to tremble. The telephone rang.

'Hello?' Mateo answered it.

'Compañero Mateo? Put Don Ignacio on.'

The clerk passed the telephone to his boss.

'Compañero Fuentes? Moran from the Peronist Youth speaking. We wish to convey our solidarity with your struggle.'

'Come here and fight with me then.'

'We're in permanent session. If the meeting so

decides, we'll be there.'

'OK, then go to the square and join up with the road gang. Try to seize the loudspeaker.'

Ignacio put the phone down. A burst of machine gun fire blasted the front of the building. One bullet sped through the window, smashing the thermos on the table.

'On the floor,' the corporal shouted. 'Let me out of here,' Comini wailed from the toilet.

Ignacio crawled over to the other window and opened the shutter. The Inspector tripped as he was running towards the police van and fell headlong onto the road. Three men started shooting from the roof opposite. Ignacio and the corporal ducked. The gardener fired his revolver. The bullet thudded into the front of the van just as it was starting up. It gave a lurch and stopped in the middle of the road. There followed a smash and a crashing sound.

'The road gang's arrived,' Ignacio guffawed.

The battered Chevrolet screeched round the corner with a squeal of tyres. Whoever was driving seemed to have lost control. The nose of the truck headed towards the pavement, then suddenly smashed into the police van, tearing its roof open and lifting it from the ground. It was dragged along, teetering, for several yards, then as it fell on its side the petrol tank exploded. Rossi glimpsed the sky beyond the door which suddenly opened above his head. He struggled out and ran off, his uniform ablaze. Corporal Garcia shot at him; the bullet whistled a couple of feet over his head. Rossi groaned and collapsed onto the road. The flames had reached his lapels. Eight men armed with picks and shovels ran from the square over to the Chevrolet, which had also started to burn. A fresh burst of gunfire from a rooftop forced them back to the cover of the trees. One was limping. Deputy Inspector Rossi crawled painfully towards the pavement held by the police; he fought to pull his blazing jacket off. From a doorway a policeman threw a bucket of water at him. The bottom of the bucket banged against Rossi's head, and the water emptied onto the road. Half-crazed, Rossi squirmed desperately and rubbed his back in the water. He was beating at his trousers with his helmet to try to stifle the flames.

'I don't like the look of this,' said the Inspector. He had hurt his elbow and torn his jacket sleeve in the crash.

'We can't back out now, Ruben. We have to get them out of there before the journalists from Tandil arrive.'

'Suprino said that the Mayor and the Party tribunal would take responsibility.'

'Yes, but not for this shambles. If we get them out, all well and good: if not, we're screwed.'

'Let's go in shooting then.'

'Hang on. Let the others do the shooting, then clear off. You've got to keep your hands clean. Suprino said you're going to be made police chief in Tandil.'

'There must be thousands of Commies there.'

'The place is crawling with them. In the university, in the steelworks; you'll have lots of fun.'

'Hey, Guzman,' the Inspector whispered, with a knowing smile.'

'What?'

'Remember when you fought against Perón?'

'Oh no, I was never actively against him. I simply wasn't Peronist in those days, but now I am — because Perón himself has become a democrat. That's why.'

Suprino and Reinaldo drove up in a Ford Torino. They stopped well away from the fire, then walked over to Llanos and Guzman.

'What's going on?' Suprino wanted to know.

'Ignacio's being stubborn,' the Inspector said.

Suprino stared at the flames licking over the vehicles and spat forcefully.

'He was the one who messed things up. I've talked to the Mayor. He's sending ten more men. The high-ups want a quick, clean job. Finish it tonight, then tomorrow morning they're off to the beach. One thing though, we've got to have a few police wounded. To show the journalists.'

'How can we do that?'

'Get them to attack the building, they're sure to get shot up.'

'Send them to their deaths, you mean.'

'Come on, don't exaggerate. All we need is a couple of scratches. I'll give them the order on your behalf.'

Moran and two other youths, barely more than twenty years old, appeared at the street corner.

'Inspector Llanos!'

'What is it? Clear off, or you'll be in trouble too.'

'The Peronist Youth meeting has issued a statement.'

'Oh, yeah? And what does it say?'

'I'll read it to you if you like.'

'Don't bother. Leave it with Rossi; you're all under arrest.'

'Arrest, my arse!'

'Filthy Communists! Rossi!'

'Beat it!' Moran shouted to his companions.

The three of them ran off to the square.

'Here I am, Inspector,' said Rossi. His scorched uniform was in tatters. He was dragging his right leg.

'Prepare to attack.'

'I'm wounded, Inspector sir.'

'Wounded?'

'I caught fire.'

'How on earth did you catch fire?'

'I was in the van when it went up in flames.'

'Trying to skip out, I'll bet.'

'No, Inspector; just watching the rear guard.'

'Never mind. Now you can attack.'

'I have to get some first aid, sir. A spot of ointment and I'll be fine.'

'Forget it. Take it like a man.'

'It hurts.'

'Grin and bear it.'

'But I got my whatsits singed.' Rossi paused. 'And I've another man injured.'

'Someone else?'

'Antonio. He got hit by a stone as he was cycling past the square. He fell off and cut his knee.'

'Aha. Both of you are to stay here and put up with it like real men, at least until the reporters get here from Tandil. Now, prepare for the attack. How many of you are there?'

'Me and three others.'

'OK. You're to crawl up to the Town Hall and lob in a gas cartridge.'

'We haven't got any.'

'Ask one of the Tandil boys for it — that blond fellow in the yellow shirt, or any of those with an arm band. They'll follow behind you to cover your backs.'

'Why do they have to cover our backs if the enemy is in front of us?'

'I reckon you're shit-scared.'

'They'll shoot the living daylights out of us. Don Ignacio's in a real temper today.'

'Are you a bunch of fairies, or what?'

'No, Inspector.'

'Then do as I order.'

The Inspector took off his grimy helmet and wiped the sweat with a handkerchief. He watched Rossi limping away as though one leg had suddenly gone stiff. He saw Suprino standing by the smouldering van. He called him over. The Party Secretary walked up. He had a handkerchief over his face like a cowboy, and was carrying a sawn-off shotgun.

'I ordered Rossi to storm the Town Hall,' the

Inspector said. 'What d'you reckon?'

'Good idea. The boys from Tandil are playing up. They were told in the Union it was a bit of strike-breaking, nothing like this.'

'Send some of them with Rossi, and a few more up on the roof, so they can get in from the back.'

'I'm not sure they'll play along. They're a bunch of know-all brats.'

'Then hand out a few sweets, that might win them over.'

Suprino stared at him. His handkerchief was soaked with sweat.

'Still feel like cracking jokes?'

'What about you? Why on earth did you put that handkerchief on? You look like a clown.'

'My wife gave it to me.'

'Watch out then, it might get dirty.'

Suprino walked off. The Inspector crossed the street. Guzman was tying two lengths of wire together.

'Let's see if you can get the loudspeaker working. We have to encourage people.'

'Somebody cut the wires,' Guzman explained.

A hail of road-chippings was flung at them from the corner. One hit Guzman in the back. The auctioneer doubled up, then fell on his side. He felt gingerly with one arm to discover where the wound was. The Inspector flung himself into a doorway.

Four youths ran back from the streetcorner to the square. One of the men from Tandil fired at random at the group. The gaggle of onlookers a block away vanished into their houses.

'Rossi, when are you going to attack, dammit?' Llanos shouted.

'Right this minute,' Rossi replied. 'We're going in now.'

Llanos looked around him. The van and the truck were still blazing, and the heat was peeling the facades of two houses where all the windows had been smashed. Guzman was sitting in the doorway of a house, rubbing his back against the wall. Behind the Chevrolet, the Tandil men were receiving orders from Suprino and Rossi.

'Fine,' the Inspector said to himself. 'Now they're trapped like rats.'

Inside the Town Hall, Ignacio was slowly sipping his *maté*. Corporal Garcia stood guard at one window, Moyano was at the other.

'The lads have done their bit,' Moyano said. 'We've got 'em shit-scared.'

'I reckon they're about to move in,' Garcia said. 'There's a lot of conciliation going on.'

'Consultation,' Ignacio corrected him. 'Right. Tonight's going to be tough. If the boys in the square had weapons, they could take them from the rear.'

Juan rushed in through the back door.

'Watch out, Don Ignacio,' he said, 'They're coming. Slithering along like snakes.'

Ignacio put the *maté* down on the desk. 'Let me have a look.

He pushed Garcia aside and knelt by the window. 'You're right, they're crawling towards us.'

Garcia took up his post again.

'They're bringing the Tandil gang with them. Suprino's up on the roof opposite; the idiot's wearing a mask.'

Rossi and the three policemen had crawled out from behind the burnt-out vehicles. Behind them came six of the civilians, carrying rifles. They advanced only with great difficulty, struggling to lift their heads off the asphalt. 'They'll burn their balls off,' laughed Garcia. 'You could fry an egg on that street.' A volley of shots rang out. The Inspector, posted in a doorway, Guzman and the wounded policeman from the house, and Suprino from the rooftop all fired at the Town Hall windows. The shutters and the glass were blown to bits. Moyano fell back. Everybody in the office threw themselves to the floor.

'Shit!' Garcia shouted. 'They really mean business!'

The floor was spattered with blood. There was no sign of movement from Moyano.

'Poor Moyano,' Garcia said.

He stood up, flattening himself against the wall. He poked the barrel of his machine gun out of the smashed window and fired at the group crawling on all fours. One of the policemen leapt to his feet and raced off. The others halted and fired at the Town

Hall. Bullets thudded into the office wall. The portrait of Perón swayed, then crashed to the floor.

'We've had it,' Garcia said. 'We'd better surrender, Don Ignacio.'

'No,' Juan exclaimed, 'we've still got the air force!'

'Don't try to be funny,' Fuentes chided him.

'No, Don Ignacio, I'm being serious. We've got a plane. If I can get hold of Cerviño we can still put up a fight.'

'This is no time to joke.'

'It's no joke, Don Ignacio. Try to hold out as long as possible while I look for Cerviño.'

He slipped out of the back door. Someone took a shot at him from a rooftop.

Juan sprinted across the yard and leapt over the back wall. In the street, the gang of civilians and police were still inching towards the Town Hall pavement. Two cars appeared round the corner.

'The journalists!' Suprino exclaimed.

'The Mayor!' shouted the Inspector.

The first of the cars, a Peugeot, drove up at full tilt. The driver did not spot the men in the middle of the road, and ran straight over one of them. The youngster in a yellow shirt screamed and lay still under the car when it finally halted. The others stood up and jostled the driver.

'Why don't you look where you're going, asshole?' screamed Rossi.

'Who are you talking to,' the fat man behind the

wheel asked, opening the door and jumping out. 'Who did you call an asshole?'

'You,' Rossi shouted, and threw a right hook which landed on the fat man's ample chest. The man stepped backwards and pulled out a rubber blackjack, then launched himself at the policeman, beating him over the head with it. As Rossi ducked, the fat man kneed him in the stomach. The policeman crumpled to the floor, gasping for breath. Five young men clambered out of the Peugeot. Another six got out of the other car, a Ford Falcon. They took tear-gas guns and cartridges from the back. The last person to emerge from the Falcon was the Mayor. 'Where's the Inspector?' he roared.

Back in the office, Ignacio went over to the window and glanced out.

'Guglielmini's arrived. He's brought more men.'

'Maybe they're on our side,' Garcia suggested.

'They're on their side,' Ignacio replied. 'Board up the windows while I send a message to the Mayor. Get this down, Mateo.'

The clerk ran to the Olivetti and rummaged in a drawer to find a sheet of paper.

'Write: "Mr. Mayor, I am holding you responsible for what is happening in Colonia Vela. Those traitors have killed Moyano, the gardener, and if they want a fight, they'll get one. Perón or death." '

'Who's going to take the message?' Mateo asked

fearfully.

'Comini. Let him out.'

Mateo asked Garcia for the key, and opened the toilet door. When he heard no sound, he peered inside.

'Oh, sorry,' he stammered. He slammed the door shut and looked blushing at Ignacio.

'He'll be right out,' he said.

Comini appeared a minute later, doing up his fly. Garcia told him: 'We're setting you free. You're going to take a message to the Mayor. Wave this white hand-kerchief when you step outside.'

'Which one is the Mayor?'

'That tall old man in the blue suit.' He pointed him out through the window.

Mateo gave him the piece of paper. Comini slowly eased open the door, waved the handkerchief, then stepped out. All the weapons were trained on him.

'I've got a message for the Mayor,' he called out, walking towards the group with his hands in the air.

Guglielmini read the note.

'Someone killed! You've made a real mess of this, Llanos!'

'It was them who shot first. Several of my men are wounded.'

The Mayor pulled out a notebook and a pencil. Leaning on the Peugeot roof, he wrote: 'Mr. Leader of the Council, You are accused of being an infiltrator and a subversive. Offer your resignation, and your case will be heard by the Party Tribunal. Perón or death.' He handed it to Comini. The policeman

29

walked back over to the Town Hall. He knocked on the door. Corporal Garcia opened it. Comini gave him the note and remained standing by the door. Ignacio read the message.

'The bastard. He's going to have to haul us out dead. Mateo, type this.' The clerk returned to the typewriter.

'Write: "Go fuck yourself. Perón or death." Give it to Comini and bolt the door.'

The Mayor was standing in the doorway of the Union office with Suprino, Llanos, Guzman and Reinaldo when he got the message.

'What does he say?' asked Guzman.

'Just insults me.'

'I think you should appoint a new Council Leader,' Suprino said.

'I can't yet. You've botched it. If Llanos had arrested Fuentes, you could have taken it on for the time being. But now things have gone too far. The papers are bound to play up the dead man.'

'What should we do then?'

'I'll send one of the boys from my group to put guerrilla propaganda and weapons in Moyano's house. Llanos, you announce over the loudspeaker that Fuentes was supplying them arms. Tell the reporters that too. Put a bomb in the Union doorway and then arrest two or three Peronist Youths. We've got to make it look convincing. Be quick about it. You,

Suprino, get two of the boys to shoot up my car. The rest can take care of Fuentes and the others. Let's get on with it.'

They moved off. The Mayor gave instructions to his companions. As they were approaching the police barracks they heard an explosion.

'You'll have to give me a grant to repair the building,' Reinaldo grinned.

'What do people here make of Fuentes?' Guglielmini asked.

'Er . . . . I'm not sure. They won't swallow the bit about him being Communist though,' Suprino answered.

'Fill the town with leaflets tonight accusing him of being a queer, say he spent his time in orgies in Tandil, and that his wife was always running around with other men.'

'Jesus Christ,' the Inspector shouted. 'Look at that!'

Somebody had scrawled on the front of the police station:

SUPRINO AND LLANOS ARE DEAD
THE PEOPLE WILL HAVE THEIR HEADS

'Smart-assed brats. They chucked stones at us earlier,' Llanos said.

'They think they're so clever, the punks.' Suprino said. 'That comes from being too soft on them.'

They had arrived opposite the Town Hall. Four people in a Ford Torino were waiting at the street corner. Suprino walked over to them.

'What do you make of it, Señor Luzuriaga?'

'It's got out of hand.'

'You agreed to this, didn't you?'

'We agreed to getting rid of Fuentes, but we can't support you publicly if you mess things up.'

'Talk to the Mayor.'

'We've got nothing to talk to him about. We discussed everything with you at the proper time. If this hasn't been settled by tomorrow, the Landowners' Association is washing its hands of the whole affair.'

'Everything will be fine.'

'What was that explosion?' asked Luzuriaga.

'Some Peronist Youths put a bomb in the Union office.'

'Have they been caught?'

'They soon will be, don't you worry.'

The Torino pulled away. Suprino went back to the Inspector and the Mayor. Llanos looked at his watch. It was seven in the evening. He felt tired. He thought that things really had gone too far. He could sense people watching him from behind their shutters. When all this was over he'd be transferred to Tandil. He'd always wanted to live there. About thirty people were ranged in front of the besieged Town Hall. Fuentes would have to come out, he couldn't be so pig-headed.

'If he stays in there he'll have the gardener's body rotting on him,' he said to himself.

They stopped alongside Guglielmini's Peugeot. There were five bullet holes in its doors.

'We'll soon sort things out,' the Mayor said. 'I'll set up my office in the provincial bank.'

'Why not come to the police station?'

'No, it isn't the right moment. Keep me posted. Did you see what they did to my car?'

'Señor Guglielmini.'

'What?'

'You wouldn't leave me in the lurch, would you?'

'What d'you mean?'

'Oh, nothing,' Llanos paused. 'I mean, you will back me all the way, won't you?'

'Oh, come on.'

'No, don't get me wrong. It was Fuentes who gave me this job. I've never bothered with politics. All I want is to get promoted and to move to Tandil. My wife wants the kids to go to university there.'

'Of course.'

'Inspector.'

Deputy Inspector Rossi came running towards them. His head was bandaged.

'There's a plane coming, Inspector.'

'A plane?'

'Over there,' Rossi pointed west. They could hear the sound of an engine in the distance. They all peered towards it. The old aircraft looked smaller silhouetted against the sun.

Its engine was spluttering. It flew by a few hundred feet above their heads.

'Cerviño,' said Reinaldo.

'Who?' the Mayor asked.

'The crop duster. He sprays the crops with insecticide. Always drunk.'

Cerviño eased back the throttle and let Torito glide out towards open country. Then he banked and headed back towards the town.

'Go in low and we'll give them a dose,' Juan said. 'This is going to be fun.' The propeller was creaking, crying out for oil. The exhaust spat flames. Cerviño lined the plane up with the main street and dropped to two hundred feet.

'Lower still.'

He brought Torito down to under a hundred feet, above the cars and people gathered opposite the town hall.

'Now!'

Juan released the lever. A clinging grey mist descended over the crowd staring up at the plane.

'Shit, long live Perón!' Cerviño shouted.

The Mayor stumbled over the body of a youth wearing sun glasses and fell headlong. The asphalt scorched his palms. What felt like a cool gentle dew was settling on his head. He started to sneeze. Rossi dived into a doorway. He banged his head on the machine gun that a fat man in a check cap was carrying. His wound began to bleed again. Guzman the auctioneer threw himself underneath the Peugeot. Two of the men got into the car, and started off at full speed. Guzman felt its whole weight run over his right hand, and a stabbing pain shot the length of his arm. When he saw the blood spurting from his crushed fingers, he felt sick, and then fainted. The plane was back for another run. The Inspector had taken refuge under a tree in the square. He took aim at the aircraft and pulled the trigger. At the same instant his vision clouded over, he was aware of a metallic echoing sound inside his head, and he dropped to his knees. Then he nosedived into the grass. Two members of the roadgang grabbed his arms and dragged him off into the trees.

Ignacio leaned out of the window and caught a policeman blindly trying to escape along the Town Hall pavement. He clouted him with the barrel of his shotgun, and watched him collapse in a heap. His eyes were smarting from the DDT still floating in the air. The men scattered the length of the street could not stop sneezing.

Corporal Garcia blocked off the windows again.

'We're really giving it to them now, Don Ignacio. Cerviño's a wizard.'

Fuentes flung himself into the visitors' chair and stared at Moyano's body, concealed under sheets of newspaper.

'What now?'

'What d'you mean?' asked Garcia.

'What's going to happen next? What will Perón have to say?'

'He'll be proud,' the Corporal said. 'Maybe he'll appoint me Inspector.'

The first time the plane flew over, Guglielmini had taken cover under the charred remains of the two vehicles. As he crawled under their chassis, his suit got progressively blacker. His face and hands were also filthy with soot. He looked round, and saw two of the men he had brought with him beneath the wreck of the Chevrolet. He crawled over to them. One, with dark hair and tiny eyes, cradled an enormous shotgun. The other, brown-haired and with a pointed nose, was busy wiping his face with a handkerchief, but only succeeded in getting it dirtier still.

'What the fuck have you got us into?' the darkhaired man asked. 'This isn't a proper job!'

Nearing them, Guglielmini could feel one of his trouser legs ripping as it caught on the van's exhaust.

'It's tough going,' the Mayor replied. 'We'll have to wait for nightfall to attack.'

'If they don't poison us first,' grunted the man, still scrubbing away with his handkerchief.

'I can get him the next time he comes back. I'll blow him out of the sky.'

The sound of the aircraft engine died away to nothing.

'He must have gone to load more DDT,' the

Mayor muttered.

'He's not got much daylight left. He's had it after nightfall,' the dark-haired man said.

They crawled out of the wreckage. Guglielmini coughed and spat. The street was deserted. The sky had turned a coppery red, with the sun hanging low on the horizon. The heat seemed to be concentrated in this one spot as in an oven.

They walked to the corner of the square. The Mayor's ankle was bleeding under the torn trouser leg. The dark-haired man slung the shotgun over his shoulder, took out his dark glasses, then tossed them away when he saw they were broken. A shot rang out. He felt the force of it lifting him from the ground. Flattened, he choked back the pain, which by now had run right up his spine. He struggled upright, and looked all over his body for the bullet hole. He found it in his left knee. When he saw Guglielmini and his friend scurrying off, he started to cry.

'Got him, Don Ignacio! Hit him in the leg!' Garcia shouted.

When the policeman pulled in his gun, Fuentes peered out through a crack in the board.

'You've got a good aim, Corporal,' he said. 'We're going to need it.'

Ignacio crossed to the w.c. He locked the door, lowered his trousers, and sat down. He needed to think. He knew they would never last out the night.

They wouldn't be able to leave the building, because the others would be keeping watch from the rooftops. Still, they couldn't close in as long as he and Garcia had their weapons. What would happen when their ammunition ran out?

He looked at his watch, wound it up. In less than an hour, the plane wouldn't be able to fly between the houses. At any rate, Cerviño had done a good job. Fuentes concluded that they didn't have many options. At night, in the darkness and with no witnesses, they had no chance of surrendering. He wondered where all the townsfolk had got to, why they hadn't come to his aid. He pulled the chain, and watched the water flushing inside the bowl. He went over to the mirror and squeezed a pimple on his nose. He opened the door and went back into the office. Mateo was slumped on the floor. He looked completely forlorn.

'I never dreamt this could happen, Don Ignacio,' he said.

'Me neither. How about serving us some *maté?*'

Two men from the roadgang dragged the Inspector over to the thicket of trees in the square. Then with the help of two youths they dragged him onto the pavement outside the cinema. An ambulance pulled up, and they loaded the body on a stretcher. Five men climbed in with it; another got in next to the driver.

'Where are we taking him?'

'To the railway station cellar.'

The ambulance made its way sedately out of the town centre. After the last of the buildings, it turned off along a dirt road. Llanos had come round, but couldn't take in what was going on. It was as though he was assailed by too many dreams at once. He saw the revolver pointing at his face. Then he looked at the others. Filthy, in worn-out trousers and hooded, they all carried machine guns. One kept spitting close to his legs.

'What's going on?' Llanos raised his head. 'Where are you taking me?'

'Prisoner of war,' said the youth who had his gun levelled at him.

'What war?'

'This one.'

Llanos let his head fall back on the edge of the stretcher. It hurt a lot. For the first time he had serious doubts about ever becoming chief of police in Tandil.

The aircraft glided in over the field, touched down on the sparse grass, and taxied over to a hangar. Cerviño and Juan jumped down. Juan took a long drink from a bottle, then passed it to his friend. Cerviño thrust the bottle into his mouth, and as he drank glanced up at the sun setting behind the flat line of the plain's horizon.

'To top it all, we're in for rain,' he muttered; then he looked over at Juan. 'Fetch the petrol can.'

Juan ran to the hangar and came back with the

fuel.

'There's about ten litres,' he said.

'Shit, that's not much.'

'There's no DDT left,' Juan added, as he poured the petrol into the aircraft's tank.

Cerviño calculated that ten litres would be just enough for a quick flight, if he landed in a field closer to town. But it wasn't worth it.

'I'm going to fly in the dark,' he said.

'You're out of your head.'

'Listen. Take the bike back to town. Tell the people in the Town Hall street that when they hear the plane they're to switch all their front lights on, so I can see my way along the corridor of light.'

'You'll only hit the power cables.'

'Think I'm a novice at this game? We're going to die laughing, Juan, you'll see.'

'Didn't you say it was going to rain? It's madness, friend.'

'Don't worry. After you've told everyone about the lights, go to the Town Hall and hold out there. When it's the right moment, get Don Ignacio to switch the street lights on and off three times. Then I'll come in.'

'What are you going to drop?'

'Shit. I'm going to cover them in shit.'

'Fantastic!' chortled Juan, slapping his friend on the back.

'Mind you don't puncture my bike,' Cerviño said, walking off to the hangar.

He returned to the aircraft with a shovel and ten sacks. He switched the engine on, took Torito out to the far end of the field, taxied back and took off. Cerviño was sure Rodriguez the pig-man would be delighted to have his sty cleaned out for nothing. He'd probably even let him have twenty litres of fuel. He felt for the bottle under the seat, but Juan had gone off with it.

'Drunken bastard,' he said, and shut the cockpit window to stop the wind whistling in.

As soon as he got to the bank the Mayor had a shower. Suprino had brought him one of his suits, a shirt, and a change of underwear.

Guglielmini let Reinaldo bandage his wounded ankle. When he was dressed, he sat down at the desk. A young man with a thin moustache wearing a yellow armband on his right shirtsleeve served some coffee. Guzman came in. He had an arm in a sling. There was a dark stain of blood on his bandaged hand.

'The reporters are here. They're taking pictures of the street. One of them wants to interview Ignacio in the Town Hall.'

'Put them under police protection. They're not to go near the Town Hall. And they're to leave all their cameras here. I'm going to hold a press conference.'

'I'll tell the Inspector,' Guzman said.

'Where's he got to?'

'Don't know. Wasn't he with you?'

'No. Tell Deputy Inspector Rossi then. Get the Tandil boys to surround the Town Hall so nobody can get near it.'

Guzman went out. Guglielmini lit a cigarette and looked around.

'You know what the story is. Communists, weapons, the bomb in the Union, the attack on my car, how I only escaped thanks to the grace of God. Got it? I'll do the talking.'

Five minutes later, the journalists filed in. The Mayor stood up and smiled a welcome. He could feel Suprino's suit binding him between the legs.

'How are you, fellows?'

There were four of them; they said they were fine. The young man with the moustache gave them coffee. Three of the reporters got out pens and paper; the fourth switched on his tape recorder. Guglielmini began his speech. When he'd finished, he waved at them complacently:

'Ask any questions you like. You all know me, I used to be a journalist myself.'

'Do you think the government will have to take over?'

'No,' the Mayor answered. 'The provincial government, with whom we are in complete agreement as regards the defence of Peronist orthodoxy, is well aware that we are engaged in a struggle against the forces of international anarchy, which in Colonia Vela are led by the Council Leader and a group of so-called Peronist Youths.'

'Do you think so much police violence is necessary?' one of the reporters asked.

'There has been no police violence. It was the Marxists who attacked our officers. We even have reports that Ignacio Fuentes killed a poor gardener, a municipal employee, when he refused to fight against what he considered the authentic Peronist authorities.'

'Could this mean the military will be brought in?' the man with the tape recorder wanted to know.

'Certainly not. The armed forces respect the authority of the elected government, and would only be called in if there were a serious uprising. There is no question of that here, since the Marxists are a tiny minority. The police and some ordinary citizens who are helping them in their task will have restored law and order before the night is out.'

'What's that smell of DDT?' another reporter asked.

'We had a drum of it on the truck. It exploded.'

'DDT doesn't explode,' the journalist retorted.

'It did this time,' Guglielmini replied. 'Now you can go back to Tandil. Tomorrow I'll issue a detailed statement.'

'I'm going to hang around for a bit,' one of them said. 'It's a good story.'

Guglielmini stared at him, put out.

'Very well, but don't go near the Town Hall. I don't want any wounded journalists. It's me who's responsible for you here.'

'One last question,' said the reporter with the

recorder. 'Who are those armed civilians out in the street?'

'I've already told you. Loyal Peronists who have spontaneously offered the police officers their support. Workers willing to give their lives in defence of our people and our leader.'

'Naturally,' the reporter said, staring at the yellow band on the arm of the youth who had served the coffee. 'Can I speak with Fuentes' or Mateo Guastavino's wife?'

'They can't see anyone at the moment.'

'What about the gardener's wife?'

'He was a widower. May he rest in peace.'

PART TWO

With love, with hate,
but always with violence

—Cesare Pavese

NIGHT fell, sultry and overcast. A certain smell in the air, mixed with the heat still rising from the asphalt, promised rain. Gazing at the gathering rainclouds through the skylight of the w.c., Ignacio wondered how rain could help them.

'Not even God,' he said to himself, 'not even God can save us.'

Mateo had rescued the photo of Perón in military uniform from among the bits of shattered glass. He propped it on the desk. Corporal Garcia, still watching for any movement in the street, spotted a figure crossing to the Town Hall.

'Don Ignacio,' he warned.

The Council Leader ran to the window and peered out of the crack.

'It's Pelaez, the madman,' he said.

The figure lurched up on to the pavement, stared for a moment at the pitted facade of the building, then continued. There was a banging at the door.

'Keep watch while I open it,' Ignacio said.

He slid back the bolt and turned the key twice.

Crazy Pelaez slipped in. He looked about fifty. His face was all but hidden behind a beard and moustache. If his stare had not been so intense, his eyes might have seemed gentle. There was a carnation in the buttonhole of his tattered, filthy, black jacket. He was without a shirt, and a mat of grey hair stood out from his weatherbeaten skin. He was trailing what once had been a pair of brown trousers. His shoes, though, were so smart they contrasted oddly with all the rest of his attire. He was coated from head to foot in white dust.

'Cigarette,' he requested in a slurred voice.

Ignacio took one out and gave it to him. Then he lit it. The madman smiled, and drew heavily on it.

'I was bombed,' he said.

He started to tremble. The cigarette slipped from his grasp. He covered his face in his hands, and began to sob. Ignacio felt sorry for him. He was astonished he could still feel pity for someone else. He had seen Pelaez wandering aimlessly about the town hundreds of times. The madman would stop and write strange slogans on walls and houses. He slept out in the square or under the corrugated iron in the Highways depot, or even in doorways. No one had ever seen him eat.

Now he was standing there, bathed in light. He bent down to pick up the cigarette, and had difficulty reaching the floor. For a split second, all the three men's attention was focused on him. Stooping, Pelaez had spotted Moyano's body under the newspapers. He went over, lifted one of the sheets, and stared at the dead man's face. He burst into tears again. He knelt down to embrace the body, then hugged it to him. Ignacio could see the carnation being squashed against the gardener's nose.

Two shots sounded in the distance. Garcia squinted out at the street, but could not detect any sign of movement, apart from the swaying street lamp that threw patches of light and shadow on to the house facades. Pelaez's sobs were the only sound inside the office. Suddenly, as if all his grief were exhausted, he fell silent.

'He used to let me sleep on a bench,' he wailed. He glanced over at Garcia. 'Whenever I was in jail, you put me under the tap. You're a bastard. Moyano was a good old man.'

His gaze wandered round the walls until he saw the crucifix. He shambled over to where it hung behind the desk, and crossed himself.

'Our Father which art in Heaven, Hail Mary full of grace, the Lord be with you.'

'That's all we needed,' Garcia moaned.

'Why did you come here?' Ignacio asked.

'To bring a note Juan gave me. He said it was a message for Don Ignacio.'

He searched his pockets.

'I've lost it. I threw it away.'

Ignacio looked at Mateo.

'What can it have said?' Mateo wondered.

'Things. Secrets. He told me they were secrets, that's why I threw it away.'

They all stared at him anxiously.

'I was bombed,' he said, starting to tremble again.

'Who by?' Ignacio asked.

'The Lord. God is punishing me.'

'Yes, but where did he punish you?'

'In the Union office. Nobody ever gives me anything, because I'm mad. Moyano was the only good one — that's why God punished him.' He wiped his nose on his sleeve.

'So you were in the Union office?'

'Yes. I was asleep. The earth shook, God save us. I ran out. Then Juan gave me the note with the secrets. Don't breathe a word to anyone, he said. Who am I going to tell anything to, eh? I ask you, who?'

'The message was for us,' Ignacio prompted him.

'Yes. Poor Moyano, he gave me a flower this morning. I was going to pinch it anyway, but he was glad to give it to me.'

'Don't you remember any of it?'

'The light. Let the light shine on each and every one of us.'

'Jesus Christ!' Ignacio exploded. 'Sending a message with a lunatic! Would you believe it?'

'Can I sleep here?'

'No,' said Ignacio. 'There's going to be shooting here — bang, bang! Understand?'

'Shooting? I sleep soundly. I'll sleep with Moyano. He used to let me sleep.'

At two in the morning, Guglielmini ordered the

attack. Suprino led a group of six armed men, Rossi four policeman, and Reinaldo a further half-dozen of the men from Tandil. Within half an hour they had blocked off the Town Hall street with a roadroller, two tractors and a bulldozer. All the houses were in darkness. Only the street lighting cast a feeble glow over the scene. The men spread out behind the machines. The only sounds were their hurried steps, the click of shotgun hammers, and the snapping of machine gun magazines. It was almost half-past two when Suprino gave the order to fire. The deafening roar of the shots was followed by a flash of lightning and a thunderclap. The front wall of the Town Hall withstood the onslaught, but the boards over the windows were blown away. A second volley of machine gun fire shattered the door and left a gaping hole out into the night. The first drops of rain began to fall on Colonia Vela.

The office was shaking like a cardboard box. Corporal Garcia flattened himself against the wall by the window; Ignacio threw himself to the floor; and Mateo hid in the w.c. As the door splintered to nothing, Palaez got to his feet.

'They're the ones who killed Moyano,' he said. 'Give me a shotgun.'

The corporal hesitated.

'Go on,' Ignacio shouted. 'Give him Comini's.'

Pelaez took the weapon. All he knew was that he had to pull the trigger.

'Get down on the floor,' shouted Ignacio, crawling

51

over to the other window.

Bullets thudded into the walls. Black night was visible through the smashed boards, with far off the brief flashes from machine guns. Pelaez got on all fours and crawled forward. When he reached Ignacio, he lifted his head to window level. A bullet ripped off his right ear. Pelaez did not even notice it: he stood up and fired blindly. The report was followed by an explosion. He had burst a tyre on one of the tractors. The recoil from his shotgun knocked Palaez backward onto the seat of his pants. Just as he was picking himself up, everyone on the bulldozer opened fire. The blow in his chest sent him sprawling. Corporal Garcia pushed his machine gun out of the window and fired one burst, then another. Pelaez struggled to his knees. His chest was a bloody mess, and his scalp dangled over his eyes. He groped for Ignacio's machine gun. The Council Leader placed it in his hands. The madman tossed his scalp up out of his face, and blood spattered his back. He crawled to the hole where the door had been, and went on out. The rain cleared his sight. He had time to fire off the gun before another burst lifted him from the ground, almost jerking him completely upright. Then his body fell spreadeagled on the pavement, his hands dangling in the gutter.

Torito wheeled along sluggishly. Overloaded, its bald tyres sticking to the damp ground, it trundled across the field of oats. Cerviño tried to lift off. Throttle full back, the plane rose twenty feet, then dropped to the ground again, its fuselage creaking. The countryside was completely dark. A hundred yards away, the light in Rodriguez the pig-man's house shone out, saving the pilot from feeling utterly overwhelmed by the lonely emptiness of the pampa. Cerviño figured that the wire fence must still be a good distance away. He waited for another lightning flash to confirm his calculation. The rain on the aircraft engine produced a screaming sound like a thousand barn owls.

A roaring filled the distance. One flash, a second long, was enough to show him he'd been wrong about the fence: it was barely fifty yards from him. He turned the plane back the way he had come. Its fuselage was vibrating from the wind and the straining engine. He pulled a bottle of gin from a bag, and drank until he was gasping for breath. Another flash enabled him to make out the horizon. He smiled, and stroked the plane's control panel.

'You can do it, Torito old thing, come on now.'

He gave it everything. The wheels skidded, then accelerated over the oats. Just before the wire, Torito lifted off; it climbed two hundred feet, then lost height. Cerviño panted. The whole length of the fuselage shuddered, then straightened, as if galvanised by his effort. The plane climbed slowly, held back by the wind. The altimeter had never worked, but from the light in the pig-man's house, Cerviño gauged he must be a good seven hundred feet up.

'I knew you'd do it, Torito!' he roared, and

reached out again for the bottle.

Juan knew that the lunatic Pelaez's memory wasn't exactly trustworthy, but decided to take the chance. After telling the first people along the street to spread the word about switching on their lights, he decided to risk another desperate gamble. He was pedalling hard with the wind at his back along the dirt road. He realised his eyes were no use to him at all. The rain and the pitch dark night reduced him to a clockwork figure. When he reached the first bend, he careered off the road and collided with a wire fence. He flew through the air, then splashed into the mud. He used a fence post to haul himself up. His feet were squelching in a ditch. All he could make out were the vague outlines of trees and dark clouds. Rain stung his face and his body beneath his shirt. He fumbled for his bicycle. 'Dammit!' he swore to himself as he tried to gain his footing in the mud. The chrome of the handlebars glinted suddenly in a lightning flash, and Juan caught sight of the Highways depot in the distance. He gripped the bicycle frame, then the saddle, and pulled himself to his feet. He realised the front wheel had buckled. He held it between his legs, tugged at the handlebars with all his might, and straightened the wheel. He got on and rode off as fast as he could.

The peals of thunder, followed by zigzagging light in the sky, made him uneasy. He was nearing the depot when he felt an excruciating blow to his right knee, and he fell to the ground a second time. Pain shot up his leg, which began to quiver uncontrollably. There was a sickly taste in his mouth, and he spat, unsure whether it was mud or blood. He groped in front of him until his fingers touched a tree trunk, then stood up.

'What an idiot, colliding with the gate like that!' he said out loud.

He bent down and laboriously squeezed through the iron bars. He walked to the depot, dragging his injured leg. The door seemed too solid, but the window, made of old, dry wood, looked more of a possibility. He searched about until he found a good-sized stone. He started to smash at the window frame, which gave way after five minutes. Juan climbed up on the sill, and jumped inside. The pain from his leg shot right up through his body as he landed. He screwed his eyelids as tight as he could. He felt for the matches in his pocket. They were damp. He leaned back against the wall, then followed it round until he reached the door. He found the light switch, and turned it on. He blinked until his eyes had got used to the brightness. The wind was blowing so hard it seemed that the corrugated iron roof would be wrenched from its rafters at any moment. He began his search. He found the sticks of dynamite, with long, dry fuses, in a drawer. He took ten. He wrapped them in a piece of canvas, then tied them with a piece of rusty wire and hung them from his belt. Next he found a flashlight made of chrome and stamped Highways

Department. Juan crawled out of the window and walked back to the gate. His leg did not hurt so badly now.

'Stop! Stop shooting!' Suprino shouted to his men.

The darkness and the sheeting rain prevented him from making out whose body it was sprawled along the Town Hall pavement. He huddled together with Rossi and Reinaldo behind the bulldozer.

'I reckon it's Ignacio,' Suprino said. 'He came out to die like a hero, the idiot.'

'How many are left inside?' Reinaldo asked.

'Mateo, Juan, and Garcia,' replied Suprino.

'They'll surrender. They've got no balls,' Reinaldo added.

Suprino looked at Rossi.

'Where's the Inspector got to?'

'He's vanished.'

'Run off, more like,' Reinaldo said. 'He's shit-scared.'

'Right, then,' Rossi said firmly, 'I'm in charge now.'

He called to a helmetless, soaking wet policeman.

'Hey, you. Bring the loudhailer.'

The man ran off, then re-appeared almost at once with a megaphone.

'We're going to tell those bastards to surrender,' Rossi said.

'Give me that,' Suprino said, snatching the loudhailer from him.

The rain was coming down in torrents; all the heat had long since evaporated from their bodies. The armed men were sheltering under the bulldozer. Despite the water streaming down the street against their bodies, some were managing to smoke. Suprino clambered up into a tractor cabin, left the door open, and spoke through the megaphone.

'Mateo! Garcia! Juan! Come on out! None of this is your fault!'

He paused.

'Ignacio is dead! Don't go on fighting for nothing.' Another pause.

'We won't harm you if you give yourselves up.' Nobody answered.

'Garcia! We'll guarantee you stay a corporal.'

Suprino squinted through the rain, but could not discern any movement inside the Town Hall. He growled an insult.

'You've got five minutes! If you don't come out by then we'll demolish the place with the bulldozer. We'll line you up and shoot you, dammit!'

He inspected his watch. They couldn't wait a minute longer. He climbed down from the cabin and walked over to the bulldozer. He crouched down to peer at the men shielding themselves underneath. One of them, leaning back against a wheel, caught his glance.

'Listen, mate,' he said, 'this is a shambles.'

'Stop complaining and come out of there; we're

going to set the bulldozer on them.'

The young man shook his head.

'You've had it, old man. We've played enough games. We're in charge now.'

Both of them stood up. The first prodded Suprino in the chest with his shotgun.

'We'll get them out, and there won't be anyone left to talk about it, get me?'

'Of course,' said Suprino, 'but don't get riled. I know what's got to be done.'

'You're an asshole. Thanks to you, we're going to catch pneumonia. We'll show you how to deal with scum like them.'

'They thought the madman was me,' Ignacio whispered.

'They've started up the bulldozer,' Garcia shouted. 'I think they're out to crush us. We'd better give in.'

'The Corporal's right,' Mateo said.

'They said I'd still be a corporal,' Garcia said.

'They'd forget that soon enough,' Ignacio retorted angrily. 'If you stay, tomorrow I'll make you a sergeant.'

'How about now?'

'All right, now. Mateo, type out the form.'

The clerk went over to the typewriter.

'They think I'm dead,' said Ignacio, 'let's let them go on believing it. You talk to them, and say you'll all surrender, but that you want guarantees. You want the journalists to be there.'

'What then?'

'You'll see, Sergeant; we're not finished yet.'

'Sergeant! From flatfoot to Sergeant in a single day!'

'That's what you're fighting for.'

'Right. I'll go and tell them.'

He crossed to the gaping doorway and shouted: 'Deputy Inspector Rossi!'

There was a silence.

'Who's that?' came Rossi's voice.

'It's Sergeant Garcia.'

'Sergeant who?'

'Sergeant Garcia.'

'Come on out, yellow arse, or we'll flatten the lot of you.'

'We want guarantees. Bring the journalists!'

Mateo handed Ignacio a form. The Council Leader signed it.

'You're a sergeant now,' he said.

Garcia turned to look at the Council Leader.

'Thank you, Don Ignacio. I'll show you how grateful I am.'

'Mateo, you bring the gas cylinder from the kitchen. And a bottle of kerosene,' Ignacio said.

'What are you planning to do?'

'You'll soon see. Pray that it keeps on raining.'

Mateo disappeared into the kitchen, and returned with the cylinder and a carboy.

'Garcia, tell them you'll be out in three minutes.'

The Sergeant called out: 'Hey, Rossi?'

'What?'

'We'll come out in three minutes. Have you brought the reporters?'

'Yes, they're here.'

Ignacio and Mateo heaped files, papers, and chairs close to the hole where the door had been. The Council Leader sprinkled kerosene over it all, and balanced the gas cylinder on the top.

'Now you two give yourselves up,' he said.

'Who's supposed to give themselves up?' Garcia asked.

'You two.'

'All right,' said Mateo.

'After all this, we just give ourselves up?' the Sergeant protested.

'There's nothing else to do. If we all try to get out the back way, they'll mow us down.'

'Let Mateo surrender then. He's useless at this sort of thing.'

'You too.'

Garcia stared at the Council Leader. He smiled bitterly. His tobacco-stained teeth made him look fierce.

'What are you up to? Trying to get out alone?'

'You know I'm not going to run away.'

'Well, wherever you go, I'm going too. You don't really think they'd welcome me with open arms if I surrendered, do you?'

Ignacio looked at him and smiled. He squeezed the policeman's shoulder. Then he glanced over at the clerk.

'Go on, Mateo.'

Mateo walked to the doorway, then looked back.

'Take care of yourself, Don Ignacio,' he said.

'Of course, don't worry.'

Mateo stuck his head out, and shouted:

'This is Mateo! I'm coming out!'

'Get your hands in the air,' Rossi ordered.

Mateo raised his arms and went out. He was trembling all over. As soon as he set foot on the pavement the rain soaked his clothes. He stepped over Pelaez's body. Crossing the street, his mind turned to his daughter. The water was up to his ankles.

Two armed men came across to meet him. The sky shook with a flash that split the clouds and delayed the thunderclap. They pushed Mateo behind the bulldozer, where Suprino was waiting.

'I didn't want to stay,' the clerk said.

Suprino punched him on the nose. Mateo fell back against the cabin. One of the men hit him in the stomach with the barrel of his machine gun. The clerk slid slowly down the huge wheel. As he collapsed, he began to choke, and vomited. A red stain appeared on the knee of the man's white trousers. Mateo slumped to the ground, his head drooping on one shoulder.

'Look what you've done, you bastard! I'll finish you,' the youth bellowed. He lifted his machine gun, and brought the butt down with all his strength on the clerk's head. Mateo's hair suddenly turned red, and blood begun to pour down his jacket. Suprino barged in between the two men. The youth lifted his gun and pushed it under the Party Secretary's nose.

'Back off,' he yelled in a rage. 'Back off, or you'll get it too.'

Suprino did as he was told. He looked over at Rossi.

'Take him away. Put him in the police station.'

Rossi hesitated, seeing the man with his gun still levelled.

'You're not going anywhere,' the youth threatened him. 'Leave him to me.'

He stooped and peered into Mateo's face. His eyes were tight shut. The man took out a small flick knife, and opened it with short, sharp click. He pressed it against Mateo's throat. The tip pierced his skin. The clerk started, and opened his eyes.

'Don't...don't kill me,' he stammered. 'Ig...Ignacio is...a...alive...'

'What did I tell you?' his attacker scoffed. 'They're really having a good laugh at you.'

Suprino leaned over and grabbed Mateo by the lapels. As he shook him, the knife slid deeper into his neck.

'What did you say?' Suprino barked. 'Talk, or I'll pull your head off.'

Mateo squeezed his eyes tight shut and shuddered. A dark froth came bubbling from his lips. He spat again, but had scarcely any breath left. The slimy liquid trickled down his shirt. He made a supreme effort. His voice was completely expressionless.

'He's...he is... esca...ping...'

'Who's the dead man over there?' the man with the knife asked, pointing to the Town Hall pavement.

'Pelaez...the luna...' Mateo wanted to go on, but somehow the words failed to emerge from between his teeth.

'Pelaez the lunatic,' Suprino said.

The three stared at each other. Rossi launched a kick at Mateo's ribs. He scarcely reacted. Guzman and Reinaldo came over. Reinaldo stared at Mateo for a few moments. Then he addressed Suprino.

'What're we going to do?' he asked, worried.

'Start up the bulldozer. We're going to flatten their nest.'

'What shall I do with this one?' asked Rossi, pointing to Mateo.

'Give him his ticket.'

'What?'

'I'm telling you to give him his ticket.'

'You're crazy.'

'I said you're to finish him off, dammit! Or do you want him to squeal on all of you?'

Rossi looked at his eyes. They were gleaming in the rain. The other man next to Suprino had his machine gun levelled.

'That's going too far,' Guzman said. 'After all, it's not really him we're after. We can leave him in the police station.'

'So he can blab? There's a journalist still around, and tomorrow more will be here from Buenos Aires. We're up to our necks in this.'

'I don't like it. If you kill him, count me out. It's taking things too far.'

They stared at each other. The man pushed Rossi against the bulldozer.

'Get a move on,' he said. 'Do as you're told.'

'All right,' said Guzman. 'I'm going. I don't want to be mixed up in this.'

He began to cross the street. Everyone stared after him. As he reached the circle of light under the streetlamp, the youth called out to him:

'Guzman!'

The auctioneer turned. The machine gun burst knocked him into the shadows. He clutched at his stomach, and staggered on blindly for four steps. A second volley whipped his legs from under him. His head cracked against the asphalt as he fell. His body jerked once, than lay still. The man went over and fired from a few feet away into the prostrate form. The body rolled over, limp and disjointed.

The young man retraced his steps, and trained his gun on the group. He looked each of them over in turn. Then he stared in challenge at Suprino.

'We needed a dead body, didn't we?' he said.

No one replied. For several seconds, they stood in silence. Rossi was the first to stir.

'Here, you help me,' he said to Reinaldo. They bent down, grasped Mateo under the arms, and pulled him to his feet. The points of the clerk's shoes dragged along the ground. His head flopped against Reinaldo, who felt his stomach start to churn. They reached the tractor. Rossi propped Mateo against the radiator. His body slumped forward. The policeman drew his pistol. Reinaldo eyed him nervously. Rossi fired twice, then stood rooted to the spot, as though he were observing something remote and untouchable. Reinaldo began to throw up.

A red glow lit the street. Thick flames began to pour from the Town Hall windows. The facade exploded in a shower of bricks and wood. Suprino and the armed men sprinted for the street corners. Only Reinaldo and Rossi did not budge. The policeman heard Mateo give one last groan.

Ignacio and Sergeant Garcia crawled out into the yard. When they heard the explosion, they ran to the side wall and threw themselves down in a flower bed. The fire began to light up the sky. Ignacio caught sight of a man kneeling on a nearby rooftop. He had his back to them.

'Let's get out of here,' Ignacio said.

They climbed the wall and jumped down into the

enclosure next door. A cock started to crow as if they'd come to catch him; hens jumped blindly down to the wet earth. Garcia blundered into a white object that squawked and scuttled off. Ignacio opened a wire gate and they emerged into the yard. The house was still in darkness. They climbed over another wall, and then a hedge. Beyond it they came to a passageway that led out onto the street. They went down it. Ignacio peered round the corner of the building. In the street there were only a few cars, which looked as if they had been there for some time. The two men crept along the pavement to the end of the block. There, almost directly under the streetlamp, Ignacio could see the truck he had sold Suprino. It was parked outside the Party Secretary's house. A Ford pick-up with a canvas roof. Ignacio remembered there had never been a starter. He felt for the crank under the seat in the cabin. Then he walked round to the front and struggled to insert it. He turned it twice, three times, and the engine fired. They jumped in. The seat was soaking. Ignacio gritted his teeth, put the car into first gear, and slowly began to let out the clutch. The truck's whole body began to shudder. It was then they heard a young man's voice.

'That's far enough, gents.'

The barrel of a shotgun was pressed against Ignacio's head. Imperceptibly, Sergeant Garcia slid his right hand over the trigger of his machine gun and cautiously curled onc finger round it.

'Come out with your hands up,' the youth said.

Garcia pulled the trigger. The force of the bullets tore off the truck door. The young man's body was flung backwards, and collapsed in a writhing heap in mid-street. The truck jerked forward, then stopped.

'Turn the handle' the Council Leader shouted. Garcia opened the remaining truck door and ran to the front. He turned the handle several times. Ignacio was just thinking it had always been a temperamental engine, when he spotted the half-dozen men with their guns pointing at them. Suprino called out:

'I've had a bad day because of you, Ignacio. Better start saying your prayers.'

The bicycle climbed up onto the road, wobbled, swerved, then straightened up. Juan tried to pedal faster, but he was too worn out. He was still half a block from the square when he heard the explosion. He looked up and saw the flames leaping high over the houses. For a split second he thought the sticks of dynamite would be no use any more. He propped the bike against the first tree in the square, and made his way through the beds of poppies. One of the roadgang stepped out in front of him. Others ran over to them. Juan took the bundle from his shoulder and handed it to the first man.

'I've brought some dynamite, compañero,' he said.

'Dynamite!' exclaimed a labourer with dark, Indian features. 'Dynamite to shove up those Fascists' arses!'

Juan sat down under a tree whose foliage was so thick the rain could hardly seep through. A short paunchy man came up and handed him a bottle of wine. Juan swallowed a large mouthful. He leaned back against the tree trunk and fell asleep.

Inspector Llanos was uncomfortable. What most bothered him was his itchy head, which he kept wanting to scrape against the wall. At least, he thought to himself, whoever had left him there had chosen a spot in a corner, so it was not so difficult for him to scratch his head. His hands and feet were tightly bound, and all his efforts to work himself free had proved useless. The blindfold over his eyes was pressing too tightly on his ears, but he did manage to make out the sound of a door opening. Then he heard steps on a wooden stairway. He heard someone halt close by him and deposit a heavy object on what Llanos imagined to be a table.

'How do you feel, Inspector?' the man who'd just come in asked.

'So-so,' he replied, unhappily. His head was itching again.

'Will you have a spot of rum with me?'

'I'd love to,' said Llanos, 'I was getting a bit lonely.'

Footsteps came towards him, and the Inspector felt two rough, bony hands pulling off the blindfold. The room was dimly lit. What light there was came from an oil lamp, whose wick gave off sooty fumes. Llanos blinked for a few seconds, but then his eyes adjusted to the semi-darkness. He leaned over to rub his head against the wall, then glanced up at the man.

'This itching is driving me crazy.'

The newcomer standing there was tall and rugged. His face was covered in a woman's stocking, with two holes for the eyes. He wore a black leather jacket and a crumpled pair of brown trousers. Trails of water ran down the jacket. He shook his head, and a few drops of water splashed the Inspector.

'It's still raining then?' the policeman asked.

'Bucketing down.'

Llanos studied him.

'Are you from round here?' he asked.

The hooded figure made no reply.

'What about that rum you mentioned?'

'Right.'

The man went over to the table, opened a bag, took out a bottle, and pulled the cork. He drank, then came back to the Inspector.

'I'm going to have to give it to you like a baby.'

'Aren't you going to untie me?'

'No.'

The Inspector opened his mouth, and the man in the hood placed the bottle between his teeth. Llanos swallowed a couple of times, then spluttered.

'Sorry,' said the man, 'I tipped it too far.'

'How long are you going to keep me like this?'

'Until seven o'clock. If I don't hear any further orders, I'm to shoot you on the stroke of seven.'

Llanos shivered.

'You can't be serious! Who gave the order?'

'The lads. Until seven, they told me. If nobody arrives with different instructions. . . .'

'Shit,' said the Inspector, 'How many of you are there?'

'You're the police, you should know.'

'How should I know?' Llanos moaned, scratching his head on the wall again. 'I don't understand anything anymore.'

He tried to get more comfortable.

'They stuck me here with my arse up against a plank. It really hurts.'

'Inspector.'

'What is it?'

'I'm going to untie your hands. Only your hands, so you can scratch your head. Don't try any funny business, will you?'

'Jesus, that's really good of you.'

'Don't think it's because I'm stupid. I've got a shotgun.'

'I know. Don't you worry.'

He untied the Inspector's hands. Llanos wriggled his fingers to get some feeling back into them, then wiped the grit out of one of his eyes.

'Now I can hold the bottle.'

The man passed it to him. Llanos took two large mouthfuls, and breathed in deeply. He looked at the man silhouetted against the lamplight.

'How old are you?'

'Twenty-four.'

'You won't have the nerve to kill me like that.'

'Like what?'

'In cold blood.'

'That's the way things are.'

'Only a coward would kill a tied-up man.'

'I'll untie you.'

'All the same, it stinks.'

'On the stroke of seven, those are my orders.'

'What time is it now?'

'Three-fifteen.'

The brass knuckleduster smashed into Ignacio's jaw. The Council Leader fell against the bank accounts filing cabinet, and vaguely realised that something was cutting into his back. He felt as though he was chewing his own teeth. He could hardly force air into his lungs. He saw the boot coming towards his face. He succeeded in dodging it, but the kick struck him in the chest. The office went black for a moment, then brightness returned, though Ignacio could scarcely make out any of the objects around him. Everything was swaying to and fro. Somebody caught hold of one of his legs and dragged him a couple of yards. Then two men heaved him up onto what he thought was probably a desk. He closed his eyes, and tried to distinguish the voices mingling round his head, but found it impossible to make any sense of the noises. A shrill buzzing was spinning round inside his skull, and finally settled in his brain. He could hear a moaning sound coming from his throat. His own scream gave him a feeling of horror. He attempted to force his eyes open, but the lids seemed as heavy as lead curtains. Eventually, by gripping the edges of the desk, he managed to raise his eyelids. He saw a red, smoking tip. Solid fire pressed on his eyes. He felt as though his head were a chaos of pain which he could not fuse into a whole. He longed for death to rescue him from the nightmare.

The Town Hall started to collapse. A cumbersome fire engine arrived on the scene. There were three firemen on board, and the siren was wailing for more volunteers. The whole town appeared to be dyed a shade of pale red. The firemen had pulled their uniforms on in a hurry, and now could not unroll the dried-out hose. The fire chief surmised that if God kept on sending so much water, the building would go out of its own accord. But before then he had to isolate the houses next to the blaze. In any case, they had a serious problem. There were still crowds of people in the street, thronging the pavements and hindering their work. Eight men left the main square. They reached the corner, and mingled with the crowd of bystanders. Each of them was carrying a stick of dynamite.

72

The reporter from Tandil who had stayed on in the town after the press conference stood on the corner of the square. He was thinking that he had never seen anything like it. People shooting in the streets, men killed and wounded, and now this enormous fire. A tall young man with close-cropped hair hidden in the darkness of a porch grabbed him by the arm and pulled him out of the light.

'You're a journalist, aren't you?'

'Yes.'

'OK. Then go and tell Suprino and the Mayor to hand over Ignacio before seven o'clock. If the Council Leader isn't on the station platform by then, that's where they'll find Inspector Llanos' corpse.'

'You've kidnapped him?'

'Let's say he's a prisoner of war.'

'Who are you?'

'That doesn't matter.'

'Have the police got the Council Leader?'

'Yes. You'd better find him quickly, they're going to kill him. You saw what they did to Mateo and the other guy, didn't you?'

'Guglielmini won't let them go on killing people.'

'Who knows? Get a move on, if you want to do something useful.'

The aircraft flew over again, a few hundred feet above the rooftops. The man raised his head, as though he could see it through the house roof. When the journalist made to go, he caught him by the arm again.

'Ask them about a policeman called Garcia too. They're to free him with the Council Leader.'

'You're all out of your minds. Can't you see that if this goes on, the army's bound to step in?'

'Yes, we agree. That's why we're in such a hurry.'

The reporter walked away. As he reached the corner, all the house lights came on down the main street. The sound of the plane's engine was almost directly overhead.

Cerviño peered down at the blaze and its reflection in the aircraft windshield.

Torito was tossing about in the storm, plummeting in air pockets. He was angry with himself for arriving late. He couldn't for the life of him imagine what was going on down below. If Suprino and Llanos had set fire to the Town Hall, perhaps Ignacio had surrendered. Or had they killed him? And where could Juan have got to? The whole plan had come unstuck. It was up to him now to decide what to do. As he dived down, he could see people running to and fro opposite the Town Hall, but the reflection of the flames and the pouring rain kept him from making out clearly what was going on. Then suddenly the lights in the main street came on. Cerviño's nerves steadied. As he aimed for the start of his improvised flight path, he concluded that the bombing would be useful in any case. He slowed right down and let Torito drift along on the wind, out beyond the town. It would not be easy for him to find his way along that corridor at such a low height. He reckoned it would be even more dangerous with the blazing Town Hall so close by, blocking his view. He had to judge the strength of the wind, how high the power cables were, how far he could rely on his engine. This was the tightest scrape he and Torito had got themselves into in the twelve years they'd been together.

He turned the aircraft back the way he'd come in the darkness, and again could make out the fire in the distance. It was then that the engine started to splutter, and he saw the propeller seize up before his eyes. Torito was helpless, completely at the mercy of the wind. Cerviño calculated he was far too close to the ground for comfort. He was overwhelmed by a feeling of disappointment, as though betrayed by a close friend. 'Not just when I need you most, Torito,' he complained. He pressed the ignition. The engine started up at the second attempt, but immediately stalled. Cerviño tried again, thinking the distributor must have got wet. At that instant, Torito roared into life, and he could accelerate all the way. He slowly regained height. Cerviño thumped the instrument panel and shouted:

'I knew you'd do it, Torito!'

He lifted the bottle and took a swig.

'Here's to you,' he whooped, and splashed a stream of gin on the old control panel. 'Christ, now we're going to make them shit.'

He aimed towards the blaze, and was sucked into

an air pocket. He let Torito lose height until it was almost touching the car roofs. Then he pulled back the throttle. The porch lights flashed by crazily on both sides. Cerviño could see their reflection on the wings. He pulled the lever to open the bay, and his load began to float down, mingling with the rain.

Juan slept half an hour. At four o'clock Moran clapped him on the shoulder to wake him up.

'Get a good rest?'

His leg muscles were aching, and his eyes were sticky with a dry gum. He rubbed them, and finally managed to prise them open properly. Another man was with Moran.

'The compañero here is our leader,' Moran said.

The rain was beating furiously at the treetops. Juan struggled to his feet. He clutched his throbbing knees and stretched. He looked at the man standing next to Moran. He was wearing jeans, a striped shirt, and a rough cloth jacket. He had a revolver stuck in his belt.

'Nice work,' he said with a smile.

'All for nothing,' Juan replied, running his hands through his hair.

'Why?' the man asked.

'Where's Ignacio?'

'They've captured him.'

'See what I mean? All for nothing.'

'We'll get him out,' the man said. Juan looked him hard in the face.

'How?'

'You'll see. Want to help?'

'I could do with a drink first. I feel a bit weak.'

Moran disappeared, then came back with a bottle of wine. Juan rinsed his mouth and spat. Then he began to gulp the wine down anxiously. He had finished off half the bottle by the time he handed it back.

'What do you want me to do?'

'Put some of the sticks of dynamite in the bank. At half-past four precisely.'

'Where in the bank?'

'Climb on the roof. Next to the water tank you'll find a skylight with iron bars. Break the glass, wrap some twine round the cartridges, and when you've lit the fuses, slip them through the bars. Light them at four twenty-five. The skylight is over the toilet, right next to Guglielmini's office.'

'Right you are,' said Juan.

They walked over to the tent. Juan donned an old leather jacket while Moran put four sticks of dynamite, a box of matches, and a ball of twine into a plastic bag. Juan pushed the bundle under his jacket, pressed tight against his stomach. He shook hands with each of them, and went out. He let the rain run down his face until his head was completely clear. He looked up at the black sky. Now and then a flash of lightning picked out the clouds. All at once he stopped, felt at his belt and in his pockets, then cursed. He strode back to the tent.

'Forgot my pea-shooter,' he said.

Moran handed him the revolver. Juan put it in his jacket pocket. He left the square, walked round the block, and reappeared at the corner of the Town Hall. He slipped in among the crowd gathered to watch the blaze, with only umbrellas or newspapers to shield them from the storm. He was level with the fire engine, and halted for a moment, when he heard someone calling him. He turned around. A woman handed him his plastic bag.

'You dropped this,' she said.

'Thanks.' He stuffed the bag back inside his jacket, strapping it to his body with the belt. He walked on. When he reached the street the bank backed onto, he crept along the wall. He saw a man asleep in a car, with the barrel of a shotgun poking out of the window. Juan glanced up and down the street. It was empty. He slid over to the car door the young man with the shotgun was leaning against, snoring open-mouthed. Juan pulled out his gun and pushed it against the other's teeth. Then he forced the barrel down the man's throat. The youth woke with a start.

'Drop your gun, bright boy. Move.'

The man let the weapon slide to the floor. Juan stepped back and opened the door.

'Out!'

The youth stumbled as he was getting out. Juan stuck the pistol to his head.

'No tricks. Nice and quiet.'

'Lay a finger on me and they'll chop you to pieces, turd.'

'You don't say,' said Juan. 'How many of them are there?'

'Enough to deal with you.'

'OK, now stay right there.'

Juan went back to the car. Still keeping his gun trained on the man, he felt on the floor until he touched the shotgun. He picked it up and waved it at the youth.

'Without this you're a piece of shit. You're worthless.'

The other man gave a forced laugh.

'Throw the guns away and we'll see which of us has got guts.'

'No chance. Whoever carries these says what goes,' Juan said, poking the revolver into the other's stomach. The man glared at him, then spat out the words:

'Communist asshole.'

Juan hit him across the chin with the revolver. The youth staggered, and lifted his hands to protect his face. Juan struck him over the head again, and let him crumple forwards. Then he stooped over him and carefully went through his pockets. In one of them he found a badge.

'A cop,' he whispered. 'They're all cops.'

A bullet whizzed past him into the wall. He dropped to the ground and fired at random. He cursed himself for staying too long in the same place. He started to crawl towards the shelter of the car. A second shot raised sparks from the road and sent a shower of hot powder into his face. For a good minute, Juan pressed himself against the road surface, moving nothing but his head in search of his assailant. A burst of machine gun fire swept the street.

'Christ, there's two of them,' he said out loud to himself.

The youth he'd beaten was trying to get up. Juan didn't move. He merely lifted his revolver above his head to stop the water flooding down the street getting it wet. The man staggered to his feet. Another shot pinged into the car door.

'Don't shoot,' the youth shouted. 'It's me, Raul, don't shoot.'

He hadn't noticed Juan. When he heard another clatter of gunfire, he threw himself against the car, banging against the side and slumping to his knees. Juan thrust the revolver in the back of his neck.

'Me again, bright boy.'

Raul did not look round. He recognised the voice.

'You'll never get out of this alive,' he spluttered.

'Not me *or* you,' Juan said. 'Stand up.'

'You're crazy.'

'Stand up, I said.'

He kneed him in the kidneys. The youth straightened up, his hands in the air. He called out:

'It's Raul! Don't shoot!'

Juan used him as a shield, keeping his revolver pressed against his forehead the whole time. He steered him in the direction of the pavement in front of the bank. They had taken four steps when there was the crack of a rifle. Raul doubled up. Juan felt a dull blow to the chest which took his breath away. He followed the lifeless body to the ground, then peered up at the rooftops. He ran, crouching, to the garden of the house next to the bank. A bullet whistled close by him. The parking space went all the way down the side of the house. He ran forward. When he reached the yard he took a good look at the flanking wall. He would have to scale it to reach the bank. For the moment, he was safe from his attacker. It was four twenty-five. He grasped the edge of the wall, flexed himself, and scrambled up. From there he climbed onto the roof of the bank. He was aware of the fire and the lights as the wind and the rain buffeted him. He went over to the water tank, and found the skylight. There was light inside. He opened the bag, took out the bundle of dynamite and, protecting it with his body, lit the fuses. He kept the match against them to make sure they were well lit. He smashed the glass with his heel. It was then that he heard the aircraft engine. He looked up and searched for it in the dark sky.

'Cerviño, you old bastard!'

A nauseous cloud filled the air. Juan could feel something besides water trickling down his face. He wiped it and sniffed. He grimaced in disgust.

'Cerviño, friend, you're really dumping them in the shit!' he chortled.

'I'll be back to take care of you,' the man said. He was still holding the chain he had lashed

Sergeant Garcia across the back with. The policeman's old uniform was soaking and in rags. Underneath the torn jacket, his shirt stuck to his body. Another blow had opened a wound on his forehead. Garcia slid down the wall to the ground. His head fell forward, and some dark drops dripped from the cut to the floor. He thought one of his ribs must be broken. He was waiting for the next blow. He turned his head to look at his torturer, but he was no longer in the room. He heard the cell door being bolted, and saw the man outside, stripping off his shirt. He took dry clothes out of the locker where the policemen kept their things. He dressed, and stuffed the chain and a revolver into his jacket pocket. Then he disappeared down the corridor.

Garcia waited a long time before he dared move. Eventually, when he was sure he was alone in the police station, he struggled to his feet. He pressed his hands against the wall and levered himself upright. He recalled how often he'd refused Juan a mattress. He also thought of the night he had amused himself by hosing down Pelaez the lunatic. He'd never imagined one day he'd find himself in the same cell. He didn't move for a while, to avoid the shooting pains in his back, and slid into sleep without realising it. A voice woke him.

'Hey, Garcia!'

He opened his eyes, and looked around him without raising his head. The cell and the corridor were still deserted.

'Over here, Garcia!'

He peered up at the tiny window that gave out on to the yard. Through the bars he glimpsed Moran's face.

'What are you doing here?' the sergeant asked.

Moran pushed a black bundle through the bars.

'Get down on the floor. I'm going to blow up the wall.'

'You'll blow me up too, dammit.'

'Carry the bunk to the far wall, and get under it, as flat as you can on the floor.'

'Not likely — the roof'll fall in on me.'

'I'm only using one stick. Hurry up.'

Garcia stood up and dragged the bunk over. He pushed it against the wall, then stood there watching Moran. He was busy tying the stick of dynamite to one of the bars. Then he handed the policeman the matches.

'You light it, it's raining too hard out here.'

Garcia took the matches. He struck one, which flared and went out.

'Get on with it,' Moran urged him.

Garcia nervously struck a second one.

'As soon as the hole appears, jump out into the yard. You can reach the street from there. Go and join the people in the square.'

'If I get out alive. Wait for me, just in case.'

'I can't,' Moran replied. 'I've got another stick of dynamite to plant.'

'All right, off you go. Do you know where Ignacio is?'

'No. They've probably done him in.'

'The bastards,' Garcia growled.

'Step on it, or it'll be your turn.'

Moran jumped down, and vanished out of the sergeant's sight. The match burnt his fingers, and he dropped it. He clenched his teeth, and lit another. He held the match to the fuse, and watched as it began to burn with yellow sparks. He stood there for a second, then flung himself under the bunk. He pressed his face into the dark floor. He held his breath. As he lifted his hands to his ears to protect himself from the blast, he heard the sound of footsteps outside the cell door.

'What the hell are you doing down there, Garcia?' a young voice called.

The sergeant did not say a word.

'Come out of there or I'll shoot your balls off.' It was the man who'd been beating him with the chain.

'I'm sleeping,' Garcia protested.

He heard the sound of a gun's safety catch. He curled himself up and covered his ears in anticipation of the shot. Then an explosion tore his arms down, and lifted him from the floor. It felt as if his whole body was in a cement mixer. A heavy block of rubble fell on his back and pinned him to the ground. He struggled free. He ran a hand over his still tightly shut eyes. He opened them slowly, then crawled on half-blind. He was shrouded in a cloud of dust. He dimly heard rushing footsteps, and threw himself to the ground again. After a long while, he lifted himself to his knees. There was another dull thud, and his left arm was flung backwards. For a few moments, he lost all feeling in it. He gripped some fallen masonry with his right hand, and pulled himself to his feet. The dust was streaming out of a gaping hole that opened out onto the night. He looked around, and in the corridor could see his captor flat on his back, trapped in the twisted iron of what had been the cell door. The whole floor was littered with bricks and chunks of plaster.

'Asshole Indian,' the man spat, and fired again. The bullet sped off aimlessly.

'Go fuck yourself,' Garcia shouted. His voice was shrill, desperate. The youth could barely lift his gun, hanging limp from his right hand. Garcia tried to throw a lump of masonry at him, but his back hurt too much. He stumbled forward, and involuntarily found himself standing right in front of the other man, who tried again to raise his weapon. It was too heavy for him. Garcia kicked him in the face. The youth's body crashed to the floor. The sergeant lost his balance, and fell on his back. It was only at that moment he clearly heard the sound of rain. Someone was running towards them. He snatched up the youth's revolver and aimed at the entrance to the corridor. He fired as soon as the first person appeared. The man's shirt was drenched with blood. He tried to clutch at the wall, but toppled headlong, beside Garcia. The second man fired without taking aim. As he pulled the trigger again, the sergeant saw he could be no more than twenty. The man's face immediately contorted. He dropped his hands to his groin, and fell. The sergeant stood up, everything whirling around him. He hobbled over to the hole in the wall and fell forward. He landed in a pool of water, and for a long moment lay face down in it. He coughed, and drew his left hand across his mouth. It seemed as though a knife was tearing at his forearm. He stood up, stumbled, then straightened himself once more.

'My old woman,' he said. 'What on earth's she going to say?'

The fire chief saw a huge formless shadow loom over him. He flung himself to the ground. The hose slipped from his grasp and snaked off across the street, spraying all the bystanders, who fled in panic. The sound of the aircraft was like thunder, and for a moment everything went completely dark. A rancid stench ran everywhere. People ducked for cover in all directions. Two women fell to the ground; a boy tripped over one of them and came crashing down. Some of those following managed to clamber over the bodies, but then more tripped, and a thrashing heap of arms and legs started to pile up. A man built like a barn door dodged the mound of bodies just as the fire chief was trying to stand up. The giant's knee caught him in the chest and laid him flat. Then four pairs of shoes trampled his uniform. The fireman felt a rib creak, and wanted to cry out, but only succeeded in swallowing a mouthful of water. His colleagues had vanished, swept away by the torrent of water. Those nearest the pavements hid in porches and front gardens, or forced their way into houses. Within two minutes, the plane was already far off, but the street was strewn with bodies that slithered about or turned fantastic pirouettes before collapsing. Above the groans, a series of explosions could be heard. The fire chief crawled to the pavement. Despite the rain, the fire was gaining hold. He turned painfully over on to his back and gazed at the sky. He took out a sodden handkerchief and wiped his face.

'Sergeant Luis!' he shouted.

He heard a faint reply. Then the quavering voice came in his direction.

'Wounded in the course of duty,' the voice wailed.

'More fires,' his chief said.

The sergeant looked up. The whole sky was ablaze.

'An air raid,' he said.

The fire chief tried to catch his breath. His chest and legs ached as if he'd been through a mincer.

'Sergeant?'

'Here, Chief.'

'Can you move?'

'I think so.'

'Then sound the fire siren.'

The sergeant picked himself up and tottered over to the truck. A short man came into sight round the corner, skidding along the street towards them.

'Chief! They've blown up the fire station, Chief!' he shouted, before somersaulting into the gutter. He began to crawl across the street to where his chief lay.

'A bomb,' he said. 'We've been bombed!'

The siren began to wail, drowning everything out, including the newcomer's voice. The sergeant tried to reach his colleague to help him across the street, but the road surface was too slippery. He took four or five steps but was stuck in the same spot. A Peugeot came hurtling round the corner. Its back wheels skidded and it turned sideways on. The nearside wheels ran over the fireman's back. The bumper lifted the sergeant into the air, and his body crashed to the ground next to his chief, who was staring blankly at the scene. The car, out of control, smashed into the fire engine and exploded. The flames spread rapidly to the fire engine. A man was catapulted from the car, and landed with his arms open wide. His rigid body skated serenely down the street. A gun fell from his hand. The fire chief began to cry. He dragged himself over to the body and picked up the gun. He sat up and stared at the rooftops. Everywhere was red; the houses were crackling like cellophane crumpled in a child's hands. He lifted the revolver to his nostrils. It stank.

'May God protect them.'

He raised the gun to his right temple and squeezed the trigger.

After dropping the load, Torito felt less cumbersome. It stopped juddering and responded docilely to

Cerviño's handling. As he was pulling the plane up out of the corridor of lights, he gave a triumphant shout, but at that moment Torito caught a telephone wire with its rudder. Checked for an instant, the plane soon began to gain height and head out towards open country. Cerviño was whistling a Palito Ortega song. He felt good. Now he wanted to cycle back into town to see for himself all that had gone on while he and Torito had been in the sky. He changed course and headed back to the landing field. He began a gentle descent. He was searching for the hangar lights he had left on. He spotted them some distance away. He let Torito glide in, and estimated the distance between the start of the landing strip and the fence. He knew the ground would be one slippery puddle. He glanced at the hangar lights, accelerated, and levelled out. He smiled. He had always thought crop-dusting unworthy of Torito's talents. Three hundred feet from the ground he realised the noise of the engine was disturbing his daydreams. He turned the key and switched off the noise. He concentrated on the sound of the wind and the rain drumming on the fuselage.

'Thanks, little brother,' he said, stroking the controls.

Torito's wheels touched down, sank in the mud, then came to a halt level with the hangar door. Inside, a car's headlights snapped on, and Cerviño was caught in their glare.

89

Juan leapt down. As he was running towards the door of the house, he heard the explosion. It seemed everything around him was quaking. He dropped to the ground, and as he looked back, the wall he had climbed down finished collapsing. The rain quickly swept away the dust billowing out of the bank. He stood up and let the water wash him off as well. He unzipped his jacket and the downpour struck his chest like a cold shower. He felt good, his head clear, and his body fresh as though he had slept for a hundred hours; he smiled and walked towards the front exit. As he was crossing the garden, he noticed someone crouching down behind an old Dodge parked at the opposite pavement.

He threw himself down again, and drew his revolver. He paused. The figure gave no sign of life. He edged over to the garden wall and, with the gun at the ready, peeped over. He was beginning to get impatient. In the end he decided to cross to the next house. He crept forward, crouching among the bushes, and stood up slowly. He'd gripped the edge of the wall ready to jump when he heard the shot. The bullet tore out a brick a couple of feet from where his hand had just been. He dropped to the ground and lay there without moving. He heard a menacing sound close by him. He nerved himself to leap the wall. He tensed, sprang up, barely flicked the wall with his hands, and fell face down into the neighbouring garden.

'Don't move. Keep still and drop your revolver.'

He felt like an idiot; he should never have come

out the same way he had gone in.

He threw down the revolver. He calculated that whoever was aiming at him must be hidden behind the wall which ran along the pavement.

'Turn round, and put your hands up high.'

The voice sounded familiar to him. His heart began to pound.

'Was that you, Corporal, who nearly blew my head off?'

'Juan, Juan, you brainless clown. I nearly bumped you off, dammit!'

They stood exchanging gazes for several seconds, as if to recognise each other in the rain and dark. Then they embraced in a bear hug.

'Drunken bum!'

'Hairy-arsed cop!'

Juan thumped his friend on his wounded arm. The sergeant winced.

'Careful, that's where they hit me.'

'Let me see.'

'Don't worry, it's nothing.'

Juan burst out laughing.

'So you're still fighting?'

'What else is there to do?'

'Well, Corporal, I'm with you. Let's go and find Cerviño, then between the three of us we can make sure none of these Fascists gets away with it.'

'OK, let's go.' Garcia smiled at him. 'But from now on, call me Sergeant.'

When the glass of the skylight smashed, Reinaldo was on the toilet. Above all he wanted to sleep, but Ignacio's screams from the adjoining office put him on edge. The beating the others had given the Council Leader had been entertaining enough at first, but when one of them heated a wire red-hot in the kitchen and pressed it on Ignacio's eyes, he had suddenly felt his intestines revolt, and had to run to the lavatory.

He was trying to recover when the pieces of glass fell in front of him. A gust of wind and rain swept in through the hole and soaked the floor and walls. Reinaldo felt a renewed tugging at his bowels. He hunched over, and clasped at his stomach under his navel with both hands. He broke into a sweat. He looked at his trousers down around his ankles by the toilet bowl; they were slimy with mud and smelt revolting. He wished he was at home in his shower. He couldn't quite follow the sequence of events from the moment they decided to get rid of Ignacio up until when Guzman and Mateo had been killed. Then there was the arrival of the aircraft, which had spoilt everything. Was the nightmare never going to end? Ignacio went on moaning on the other side of the wall, and the sound wrenched at his innards. He heard noises on the roof, but couldn't work out what was going on up there. He watched as a package appeared through the skylight. The fuses were burning with the sound of blazing straw. Reinaldo's bowels protested violently. Six feet above his head, the sticks of dynamite swung to and fro like a pendulum. He reached up to catch them, but failed by inches. He shouted, but his voice merged with Ignacio's, which went on for some seconds longer. He could see how quickly the fuses were burning down; he reckoned his only chance would be to grab them and throw them in the toilet bowl. He jumped despairingly, but his feet snagged in his trousers and underpants. He fell forward, and his head banged against the wash-basin. He lay on the floor with the drizzle filtering down through the skylight, while the last inches of fuse spent themselves in front of his face. The blow had stunned him, but he made one last effort. Gripping the washstand, he hauled himself up and caught the dynamite. It scorched his hands. Quaking with fright, he flung himself over the toilet.

Ignacio stopped breathing moments before the blast. Suprino had bent to press an ear to the Council Leader's bare chest, and all the others were waiting expectantly for a sign from him. Guglielmini had got up from the sofa he'd been lying on. One of the young men was still holding the red-hot wire. The other had a cigarette which had gone out dangling from his lips. His eyes were half-closed with fatigue.

The lavatory wall was torn from its base and spewed out bricks like artillery shells. Before anyone had time to react, part of the roof caved in. A blow in the chest from a brick sent Guglielmini sprawling back on the sofa. He fought for breath, but saw the two youths disappear beneath the masonry from the roof. Huge pieces fell on Ignacio's body, but he was beyond feeling them. The shock wave threw Suprino against the far wall. The confusion was soon over. Guglielmini leapt to his feet and ran through the cloud of dust to the front door. The Mayor's Peugeot was parked in the street outside. He got into the driver's seat, and noticed the keys were in the ignition. He waited for a moment for his muscles to relax.

Suprino struggled up. He looked around him. A man's legs were sticking up out of a heap of roof tiles. He waded through the rubble, staring in consternation at the effects of the disaster. The grotesque figure of Reinaldo had his arms folded across his chest as though he were clutching something, yet he had no hands. The toilet bowl had been blown up with him, and lay filthy and split in half alongside his body. Suprino looked round everywhere, and realised that Guglielmini was no longer there. He ran over to the bank safe, and found it had been knocked to the floor. He tugged at its door, but cursed when he realised that the blast had not damaged it in the slightest. He went out into the street. Guglielmini was in the car. Suprino got in and sat next to him.

'Don't worry,' he said. 'We've still got an ace up our sleeves.'

'I've had enough,' Guglielmini replied. 'This is too much for me. We've got to get out of here, leave the country.'

'That's not going to be easy. Let me handle this.'

94

'What are you thinking of doing?'

'Playing the only card we have left.'

Guglielmini stared at him. Suprino was still quite calm.

'The Army,' he said.

The car headlamps lit up Torito's fuselage. The beams of light cut swathes across the field of oats, and the sheeting rain stood out clearly. Cerviño did not move in his seat. He knew it would be useless to try anything. Two men were pointing revolvers at him, and a third had a shotgun. They were sheltering under the hangar roof. The one with the shotgun shouted:

'Put your hands up and climb down!'

Cerviño felt no inclination to move. The drumming rain, the warmth of the cockpit, and the gin he had drunk made him light-headed.

'Go and get stuffed!'

He tipped his head back and raised the bottle. This movement worried the others.

'Get him out, Tito,' the one with the shotgun ordered.

The youth raised his gun and went up to the plane. He was already wet, but the rain that now began to run down his neck annoyed him. He opened the aircraft hatch.

'Get down.'

Cerviño hid the bottle. The youth waved impatiently for him to leave the cockpit.

'Did I mess up the town?' Cerviño asked.

'Don't play the clown, the show's over. Get out of there.'

'No. If you're going to kill me, do it here, where it's not raining.'

'Who gave you your orders?' the youth asked.

'Nobody.'

'Who?'

'I don't take orders, son. Never. That's why I'm always up aloft,' he pointed to the sky.

'Why are you defending him?'

'Who?'

'That turd. The Council Leader.'

'Because he's a Peronist and the salt of the earth.'

'You and who else?'

'Me and Torito.'

'Where is he?'

'Here,' he said, patting the control panel. 'Good old Torito. Five thousand hours flying and never so much as a hiccup.'

'You're a fool, getting yourself killed for fuck-all.'

'Fuck-all?' Cerviño looked at the young man, who could not have been more than twenty-five. 'Are you from Buenos Aires?'

'Uh-huh!'

'Get well paid?'

The youth was completely drenched. He heard his boss calling him.

'More than you,' he said.

'Fascist brat.'

'Mind your tongue, old man.'

'A daddy's boy, a stuck-up little snob,' Cerviño hummed.

'Shut your mouth, shitface. Who are you to teach me how to be a Peronist?'

Cerviño stared at him dumbfounded. He began to laugh. He lifted the bottle and took another swig.

'Hurry it up, Tito!' one of the waiting group shouted.

'Can't you see they used you, toadface? You'll never understand a thing, will you?' Tito said, cocking his revolver.

'Faggot brat. You're really brave with that thing in your hand, aren't you? Even so, squirts like you are useless.'

Tito hit him in the face with the gun. One of Cerviño's eyes spouted blood. The youth went back to his companions.

'He won't come out,' he said.

'To hell with him,' the man with the shotgun said. He stepped forward and fired. The plane's windshield was smashed to smithereens. Cerviño slumped in his seat. Tito fired at him with the revolver. The body jerked forward, and flopped on to the controls. The rain doused the blood from Torito's nose. The four men got into their car. Tito started it up. They drove off towards the road. Cerviño felt as if a blowtorch was burning his face. He couldn't see. He reached for the bottle, but didn't have the strength to lift it.

'We have to go and find Cerviño,' Juan said. 'There must be a couple of bikes in the square.'

They walked along, staying close to the damp walls. They kept their eyes fixed on the rooftops, but the whole town appeared empty. Juan realised a new day was dawning. At first he thought the red in the sky was a reflection from the blaze, but then he saw that at the far end of the street, where the fields began, the horizon looked as if it was on fire too. The rain had eased off, and the clouds were beginning to break. He reckoned it must be about six o'clock. They stopped when they reached the corner of the square. Juan pushed Garcia towards a clump of shrubs growing in the pavement outside an old house. The sergeant looked about him, and took a lungful of air. He felt better.

'Jesus, I could do with a drink.'

Juan raised his head to the sky.

'Yeah. Is your arm hurting, Sergeant?'

'It's nothing. Only a scratch.'

They ran across the street to the tiled pavement of the square. They leapt over a bed of carnations. From behind a tree, a man followed them with his gaze, keeping a shotgun trained on them. They walked across the grass, between the magnolias, to the small tent. There were five men inside, in the light of a kerosene lamp. One of them was the man Juan had met earlier. He stood up when he saw them come in.

'Who's the compañero?' he asked.

'Sergeant Garcia,' the policeman replied, and held out his hand.

'He defended the Town Hall with Ignacio,' Juan told them. 'They were captured together.'

'Of course,' the man said. 'We sent Moran to spring him from jail.'

He looked at Garcia and gave him a smile. Then he pointed to the sergeant's wounded arm.

'You're injured. Get your jacket off and let me take a look at it, compañero.'

Garcia didn't move.

'Where's Don Ignacio?' he wanted to know.

'He's dead,' the man said.

'Dead?'

'They tortured him till he died.'

'Have you seen him?' Juan asked, anxiously.

'Yes. His body was in the rubble of the bank, where you put the dynamite.'

'Oh, God...poor Ignacio,' the sergeant said. 'Have you buried him?'

'There's no time for that, compañero. We have to pull out.'

'Pull out?' Juan queried. 'Why are we going to pull out if we've got them by the balls?'

'The Army and the Federal Police are on their way.'

'We're not going to run away now,' the sergeant said.

'We're not running away.'

'Oh, no? If you run in a backward direction, what else do you call it?'

The man smiled. A lengthy silence fell. Juan asked for a cigarette. He was deep in thought. Another man came into the tent and spoke to the leader.

'We've got Rossi,' he said.

'Good. Put him with Llanos.'

The man left. Garcia looked at the man in charge.

'You've got the Inspector?' he asked.

'Yes. And now Rossi as well. He killed the clerk, Mateo.'

'Are you going to take them with you?' asked Juan.

'They'll stand trial.'

Juan stared at him for a while.

'What for?'

'How do you mean, what for?'

'What are you going to try them for? They started all this. They killed Ignacio, Mateo, Moyano, and the madman. What are you going to hand them over to a judge for? You know what trials are like in Buenos Aires. They'll be out again within a week...'

'They're not going to be tried in the capital, compañero. We're going to try them. You and us. The friends of the men they killed.'

'I don't know anything about that kind of thing,' Garcia protested.

The leader gazed at him, and smiled again.

'You don't have to know anything,' he said. 'It's not something you learn by studying. Once you've

100

killed and seen people die, you know all there is to know.'

Garcia stared down at his feet. The man asked: 'What would you do with them?'

The sergeant had puffy eyes, a dry face.

'I'm no good at these things,' he said. 'I can't discuss points of law.'

'We aren't going to discuss any points of law. The laws of the Inspector, Suprino, Deputy Inspector Rossi? We've got our own laws now.'

'I'm not sure,' Garcia said, wiping his eyes on his jacketslceve. 'But I reckon that any bastard who kills the way they murdered Ignacio...'

His voice trailed off. He looked round at them all, waiting for someone to finish the sentence for him. Nobody said a word; Garcia hung his head again, and said almost in a whisper: 'A coward like that deserves to be shot.'

He began taking off his jacket. He glared at Juan, who was smoking his cigarette slowly. He saw him nod in agreement.

'Get me another shirt, would you, Juan?' Garcia said. 'This one is sticky with blood, and the wound is hurting a bit.'

Suprino was driving too quickly for the treacherous road conditions. Guglielmini was slumped in the seat beside him. He looked a picture of despair. He'd been given precise instructions, and had failed to carry them out. The situation had slipped out of his control, and by now he supposed it was too late. It occurred to him it was Suprino who had started taking all the decisions. He wanted a cigarette, but had no matches. From time to time he shot a sideways glance at the Party Secretary. Suprino exuded resolution, sure of what he was going to do. He'd find a way to deal with the Army, he knew several of them. The problem would be how to sell such a tricky situation to them.

'They won't believe your story about Communists,' he said.

Suprino drove on in silence for a while. Then he smiled.

'I don't even have to mention it. For them, having someone like Ignacio pulling out a shotgun is like the Devil himself jumping out of his box. They don't like people shooting each other without permission. That's *their* job.'

'And Perón?'

'What about Perón?'

'He'll have our heads. We're finished, we might as well make ourselves scarce.'

Suprino pulled the car over to the side. The rain was almost over by now, and the sun was filtering through the dispersing clouds. He looked at the Mayor. He couldn't take him to Army Headquarters. He was too scared, he was a weakling. A gutless political shyster. He switched on the radio. A special newsflash was dedicated to the events in Colonia Vela. The Federal Police had despatched units to restore order following riots caused by extremist elements backed by the Council Leader. According to the latest reports, one person had been killed.

'One person killed,' Suprino couldn't help but laugh. 'Your friend's going to wish he were dead.'

'Which friend?'

'Your friend, Perón's adviser.'

The radio was playing a Gardel tango.

'What about you? How are you going to sell this to the Army?'

Suprino glanced at him. It occurred to him yet again that Guglielmini was an idiot.

'I don't need to sell them anything. They'll have to get involved in this. They've no choice. They'll follow hard on the heels of the Federal Police.'

'All right, but count me out. Do it your own way.'

'So you can shop me when we meet the soldiers?'

'No, Suprino, I'm beating it. You do whatever you like.'

The Party Secretary took out a revolver.

'Get out.'

'What's got into you?'

'Get out, I tell you.'

'You're crazy.'

Suprino jumped out of the car, ran round the front, and flung open Guglielmini's door. The Mayor threw up one arm to defend himself, and clung to the steering wheel with the other. Suprino punched him in the face. Guglielmini sprawled back. Suprino grabbed him by the hair and dragged him out. The

Mayor fell onto the roadside.

Suprino put the gun to the Mayor's head and fired. Guglielmini's body arched, then lay motionless. Suprino pushed him off the road with one foot, then toppled him into a ditch full of weeds. The body lay half-immersed in the water and mud. Suprino returned to the car, pulled out on to the road, and accelerated. Now Rivero was singing a tango on the radio. The Party Secretary sped along at a hundred miles an hour, and could feel a crosswind tugging at the car. He sneezed. Perhaps he was going to catch a cold. They would have aspirin in the barracks.

Juan and Sergeant Garcia left the asphalt road and ploughed along the muddy track. The bicycle wheels scooped earth into the mudguards, and both of them had to strain on the pedals to make any headway. The sky was tinged red and blue with the first rays of the sun. The rain had stopped, and the clouds were white again. A gentle breeze was blowing from the west. Their sodden clothes were stuck to their bodies. They felt chilled, and didn't speak.

They could see Torito from the gate. One of its doors was open, flapping in the breeze. The hangar light was still on. They got off their bikes. Juan glanced inside the shed, then walked over to the field of oats that Cerviño used as a landing strip. He went up to the plane, with Garcia close behind him. They saw the smashed windscreen and the bullet holes in the fuselage. Juan tried to run, but slipped. Juan stood there as if rooted to the spot, slowly sinking back into the mud. He lifted his hands to his head.

'They've killed him! The bastards, they've killed him!'

His voice came out as a hoarse shout. He tried to step forward, but was so glued to the ground that he fell on one side. A feeble voice reached them from the aircraft.

'Not yet they haven't, brother.'

'Cerviño!' shouted Juan, crawling on all fours, unable to lift either hands or feet clear of the mud. Garcia was staring at him, his tanned features taut with grief. Juan managed to reach the aircraft hatch.

'Pass me the bottle, will you? I can't see a thing.' Cerviño stuttered.

His face was a gaping wound, red with blood. His eyes had vanished.

'Cerviño... what did they do to you?'

The pilot stirred, propping his hands against the instrument panel.

'They were waiting for me...'

Juan searched for the bottle of gin. There were only a couple of drinks left. He lifted it to Cerviño's face. The pilot opened the hole where his mouth had been, and contrived to swallow some. Juan had the impression he was smiling.

'Jesus Christ, friend,' he murmured.

'Don't be scared,' Cerviño said. 'I can't be any uglier than before.'

His voice was hollow, strangled. Juan gave him another drink.

'I dropped them in it, didn't I?' he said, in a faint whisper.

'You did, friend. You shat on them.'

'Did Ignacio win?'

'Of course. Can you move?'

'I don't know. I'm fine as I am. I'm just a bit cold...'

'We'll get you to town so they can take care of you.'

'It's no use, I'm shot to bits...just my luck to be on the way out right now...'

'Hang on, I've got the bike here. I'll take you to the first-aid post.'

'Give me another drink.'

Juan glanced at the bottle.

'There isn't any more, friend. Last out till town, and I'll buy you a quart.'

He tried to ease him out of the plane. Cerviño groaned, and slumped to one side.

'Don't move me...we really shat on them, didn't we...are you there, Juan?'

'Yes, I'm here.'

'Tell Don Ignacio I did all I could...tell him I'm a Peronist and...tell him to keep going...when Perón gets to hear about it, he'll be real proud...'

His body heaved and collapsed. Juan ran his fingers gently through the black hair. He turned to Garcia with a glazed look.

'Give me a hand,' he said.

They carried him to the hangar. Garcia fetched a tarpaulin, and they wrapped the body in it. They left the hangar. The sun had fully risen. Juan looked enquiringly at his friend.

'Wc're not going to give up, are we?'

They walked to the aircraft in silence. Torito was tilted over, one wheel buried in the earth. It was swaying gently in the wind.

'Who are we going to fight?' Garcia asked.

'They said the Army was on its way. We can't quit now, Sergeant.'

'Can you fly the plane?' the sergeant asked.

'No...but I've watched Cerviño. It can't be too difficult.'

They walked all round Torito. The sun glinted off its wings.

'Hey, Juan.'

'What is it?'

'Are we going to win?'

'Of course. They're all a heap of shit.'

Sergeant Garcia smiled.

'And afterwards we'll go and fetch him.'

'Fetch who?'

'Perón. We'll bring him here.'

'You're out of your mind, Sergeant.'

'Why? We can show him what's left of the town, tell him all about Ignacio, Mateo, and Cerviño, all those who gave their lives for him.'

Juan stared at his friend. His eyes were swollen

and bloodshot.

'When he hears, the old boy will be really moved.'

'He'll come out and make a speech on the Town Hall balcony, and the Army men won't know where to put themselves, they'll be scared witless.'

They walked back to Torito's cockpit. Before climbing in, Juan peered up at the sun. It was so bright he had to shut his eyes.

'It's going to be a beautiful day, Sergeant.'

Garcia turned towards the town, and stood staring at the horizon. His face was weary, but his voice rang out loud and clear:

'A day...for Perón.'

Books from
Readers International

Sipho Sepamla, *A Ride on the Whirlwind*. This novel by one of South Africa's foremost black poets is set in the 1976 Soweto uprisings. "Not simply a tale of police versus rebels," said *World Literature Today*, "but a bold, sincere portrayal of the human predicament with which South Africa is faced." Hardback only, 244 pages. Retail price, US$12.50/£7.95 U.K.

Yang Jiang, *A Cadre School Life: Six Chapters*. Translated from the Chinese by Geremie Barmé and Bennett Lee. A lucid, personal meditation on the Cultural Revolution, the ordeal inflicted on 20 million Chinese, among them virtually all of the country's intellectuals. "Yang Jiang is a very distinguished old lady; she is a playwright; she translated Cervantes into Chinese...She lived through a disaster whose magnitude paralyzes the imagination...She is a subtle artist who knows how to say less to express more. Her *Six Chapters* are written with elegant simplicity." (Simon Leys, *The New Republic)* "An outstanding book, quite unlike anything else from 20th-century China...superbly translated." *(The Times Literary Supplement)*. Hardback only, 91 pages. Retail price, $9.95/£6.50.

Sergio Ramírez, *To Bury Our Fathers*. Translated from Spanish by Nick Caistor. A panoramic novel of Nicaragua in the Somoza era, dramatically recreated by the country's leading prose artist. Cabaret singers, exiles, National Guardsmen, guerillas, itinerant traders, beauty queens, prostitutes and would-be presidents are the characters who people this sophisticated, lyrical and timeless epic of resistance and retribution. Paperback only, 253 pages. Retail price $8.95/£5.95.

Antonio Skármeta, *I Dreamt the Snow Was Burning*. Translated from Spanish by Malcolm Coad. A cynical country boy comes to Santiago to win at football and lose his virginity. The last days before the 1973 Chilean coup turn his world upside down. "With its vigour and fantasy, undoubtedly one of the best pieces of committed literature to emerge from Latin America," said *Le Monde*. 220 pages. Retail price, $14.95/£8.95 (hardback) $7.95/£4.95 (paperback).

Emile Habiby, *The Secret Life of Saeed, the Ill-Fated Pessoptimist*. Translated from the Arabic by Salma Khadra Jayyusi and Trevor Le Gassick. A comic epic of the Palestinian experience, the masterwork of a leading Palestinian journalist living in Israel. "...landed like a meteor in the midst of Arabic literature..." says Roger Hardy of *Middle East* magazine. Hardback only, 169 pages. Retail price, $14.95/£8.95.

Ivan Klíma, *My Merry Mornings*. Translated from Czech by George Theiner. Witty stories of the quiet corruption of Prague today. "Irrepressibly cheerful and successfully written" says the London *Financial Times*. Original illustrations for this edition by Czech artist Jan Brychta. Hardback, 154 pages. Retail price $14.95/£8.95.

Fire From the Ashes: Japanese stories on Hiroshima and Nagasaki, edited by Kenzaburo Oe. The first-ever collection in English of Stories by Japanese writers showing the deep effects of the A-bomb on their society over forty years. Hardback, 204 pages. Retail price $14.95/£8.95.

Linda Ty-Casper, *Awaiting Trespass: a Pasión*. Accomplished novel of Philippine society today. During a Passion Week full of risks and pilgrimages, the Gil family lives out the painful search of a nation for reason and nobility in irrational and ignoble times. 180 pages. Retail price $14.95/£8.95 (hardback), $7.95/£3.95 (paperback).

Janusz Anderman, *Poland Under Black Light*. Translated from Polish by Nina Taylor and Andrew Short. A talented young Polish writer, censored at home and coming into English for the first time, compels us into the eerie, Dickensian world of Warsaw under martial law. 150 pages. Retail price $12.50/£7.95 (hardback), $6.95/£3.95 (paperback).

Marta Traba, *Mothers and Shadows*. Translated from Spanish by Jo Labanyi. Out of the decade just past of dictatorship, torture and disappearances in the Southern Cone of Latin America comes this fascinating encounter between women of two different generations which evokes the tragedy and drama of Argentina, Uruguay and Chile. "Fierce, intelligent, moving" says *El Tiempo* of Bogotá. 200 pages. Retail price $14.95/£8.95 (hardback), $7.95/£3.95 (paperback).

Osvaldo Soriano, *A Funny, Dirty Little War*. Translated from Spanish by Nick Caistor. An important novel that could only be published in Argentina after the end of military rule, but which has now received both popular and critical acclaim — this black farce relives the beginnings of the Peronist "war against terrorism" as a bizarre and bloody comic romp. 150 pages. Retail price $12.50/£7.95 (hardback), $6.95/£3.95 (paperback).

READERS INTERNATIONAL publishes contemporary literature of quality from Latin America and the Caribbean, the Middle East, Asia, Africa and Eastern Europe. Many of these books were initially banned at home: READERS INTERNATIONAL is particularly committed to conserving literature in danger. Each book is current — from the past 10 years. And each is new to readers here. READERS INTERNATIONAL is registered as a not-for-profit, tax-exempt organisation in the United States of America.

If you wish to know more about Readers International's series of contemporary world literature, please write to 503 Broadway, 5th Floor, New York, NY 10012, USA; or to the Editorial Branch, 8 Strathray Gardens, London NW3 4NY, England. Orders in North America can be placed directly with Readers International, Subscription/Order Department P.O. Box 959, Columbia, Louisiana 71418, USA.